SCROLL

RUTH HARTZLER

RUTH HARTZLER BOOKS

Scroll
Relic Hunters Taskforce Book 1
Copyright © 2019 by Ruth Hartzler
All rights reserved.

This is a work of fiction. Any resemblance to any person, living or dead, is purely coincidental. The personal names have been invented by the authors, and any likeness to the name of any person, living or dead, is purely coincidental.

All translations are the author's, apart from the Herodotus quote inscribed on the James Farley Post Office in New York City which was by Professor George H. Palmer.

FACT

"As Rich as Croesus"

This book is based on fact—the treasure of Croesus of Lydia. Croesus lived in Sardis, an incredibly wealthy city. Sardis is one of the cities mentioned in the Seven Churches of Asia in the Book of Revelation.

Croesus was indeed wealthy. Sardis stood alongside the Pactolus River which was rich in gold deposits. No one has ever found the Croesus treasure, apart from a few items. The robbery of some of those items is recounted accurately in this book. The Croesus treasure would be worth billions.

Teams from Harvard and Cornell universities

have been excavating at Sardis for years, but the site is huge and the going is slow.

All descriptions of Ephesus, Sardis, Pergamon/Pergamum, Selcuk, Oxford, and other locations, whether ancient or modern, are accurate.

The famous copper scroll, 3Q15, is one of the Dead Sea Scrolls discovered in 1952 at Qumran. However, the copper scroll of this book is fictional.

The history mentioned in this book is accurate, but the underground Temple of Artemis and the Lydian copper scroll are fictional.

There is no Temple of Artemis under the Acropolis North at Sardis—not as far as I know! Nobody knows what, if anything, is there.

There do exist several exposed sections of the tunnel that connected the Acropolis North with the dry stream-bed which once ran between ByzFort and Field 49.

Roman tunnels dug by tomb robbers under a burial mound have been discovered. It is thought the tunnels run to the chamber of a member of the Lydian royal family. Archeologists have dug over one hundred meters of tunnels but have not yet discovered the chamber.

LYDIA, 546 B.C.

GORDIAS LOOKED OVER HIS SHOULDER. THEY were closing on him. He clutched the bag of electrum coins to his chest.

He was close now, so close he could almost taste the gold.

For a minute he hesitated, weighing up his options. Did he have time to reach the tunnel? Maybe it would be better to lead the others away even though that would mean his certain death. His mission was to keep the treasure safe.

He ducked behind a boulder and looked at his pursuers.

No, they were far enough away. He would reach the tunnel without discovery.

He took another deep breath and wiped the sweat from his brow. His throat hurt and he could taste blood but was aware it was purely from the exhaustion. He was uninjured, for now at least. Gordias knew they wouldn't be able to track him over the rubble and the rocky pathway made by wild mountain goats.

As he lowered the bag of coins, he heard a noise.

Gordias ducked under a bush as a mountain goat scurried past him. Whoever was closing in on him had frightened the goat.

His only weapon was a knife, and his pursuers were bigger and stronger than he. Besides, he was vastly outnumbered, apart from the one pursuer who was rapidly closing in.

Gordias silently shuffled backward under the bush. As he did so, some scree tumbled down the rock face directly above him. It was the goat, but maybe his pursuer didn't know that. He held his breath as the man's legs came into view, as did his short sword swinging from his belt beside his left thigh. Gordias gazed on the man's ostentatious clothing with disapproval: multi-colored long pants and a bright purple and crimson cloak.

The pursuer's pace quickened and he hurried along the path to the left from where the rockfall had come.

Gordias sighed with relief. He wished to go to the right. It would be a while before his pursuer realized he was chasing a goat, if he ever did. Gordias held his breath and inched out carefully, in case the other Persians were closer. Behind the shelter of a tree, he looked out over the landscape once more. Now he couldn't see them, but he couldn't hear them either and he was certain they hadn't made up much ground. Their fancy clothes would prove a hindrance over the rocks.

With that, he hunched over and ran to the right as fast as his burden of treasure would allow him.

It was dusk now, the time of day in which it is hardest to see. Still, he knew that would hinder his pursuers as much as it would hinder him and the tunnel entrance was well hidden. He had made himself a camp at the entrance to the tunnel, a rough bed of leaves and a stash of supplies: figs, grapes, and apples, and some now-stale bread. He even had a column krater filled with wine. Lydian soldiers were as prepared as the Persians were flamboyant. A trickle of water ran down a rock and pooled at the bottom. He could live there for a while if he could catch small game from time to time.

Gordias knew the route to the entrance well, being one of the guards entrusted by Croesus himself. The Persians wouldn't find him there.

His king, Croesus, had retreated from the battle on the eastern bank of the Pactolus River to the impenetrable fortress at Sardis. Sadly, the acropolis turned out to be not so impenetrable, not in the face of Cyrus the Great and the mighty Persian army. They had taken Croesus, maybe even killed him. Just before the Persian army captured the acropolis, Gordias and other soldiers were sent to ascertain whether the Persians had discovered the treasure in various locations. Gordias was to make sure the biggest stockpile of all was safe.

Gordias's thoughts turned to his situation. He was grateful to the goat. Maybe it had saved his life. He allowed himself a small smile of satisfaction as he turned by a yellow-flowering shrub and rounded the corner.

As he made to climb over a boulder, the ground shook. Surely it wasn't an earthquake? Gordias had experienced slight earth tremors, but this seemed stronger. Besides, it wasn't as if the ground was shaking—it was as if the very air around him was shaking.

Maybe that's why the birds had been conspicuous by their absence that afternoon. Gordias heard some rocks fall and hoped they were falling on his pursuers. Still, he was sure they had all gone in the wrong direction, but more would come. What was he to do? He needed help and no help was coming. The mighty Lydian Empire had fallen.

Gordias approached his destination. Now he had to climb what appeared to be a vertical rock face and then he would be in the cave. He pulled himself up, reaching for the handholds he knew to be there and then threw himself onto the ledge. He looked around to make sure he hadn't been seen before rolling into the cave.

Gordias shimmied inside backward and then stood. He deposited his bag on the ground before stretching his shoulders and arms, sore from the burden. He lowered the bag of coins and smiled widely.

He was still shaking from his narrow escape but was hungry. He reached for a handful of figs and stuffed them in his mouth. That's when the rumbling came again.

There was a loud sound like thunder and it was as if the walls were leaning toward Gordias, closing in on him. He put his hands above his head as he heard rocks falling. Gordias threw himself back against the rock wall, terrified, as everything continued to shake.

Boulders fell past the entrance to the cave and one landed on the ledge, blocking most of the light.

Gordias looked up as the cavern roof fell on top of him.

2

THE PRESENT DAY
OXFORD

Professor Jason Hobbs slunk along the walls of the ancient Bodleian Library, looking over his shoulder in fear. His destination: the Rare Books and Manuscripts Reading Room in the Duke Humfrey's Library.

A Professor of Iron Age Greece and Anatolia, Hobbs had been in Oxford only a few days and had taken a room in the Old Bank Hotel, a short walk from the Bodleian Library. He had engaged in a spot of sightseeing to throw whomever was following him off the track. For three days, he had traipsed through the Ashmolean Museum, the Botanic Gardens, and Christ Church College where scenes from Harry Potter were filmed and where Henry George Liddell, known to most as the father of the inspiration for *Alice in Wonderland* but known to Hobbs as a celebrated ancient Greek lexicographer, was Dean more than a century earlier.

He flattened himself against the walls and held his breath. The footsteps echoing softly along the corridor stopped. Just as he feared, someone was following him now. Hobbs waited, the only sound being the beating of his heart.

The lower reading room of the Bodleian Library was the main reading room for the study of Classics and Ancient History. Hobbs knew the classical Greek section was on the north side and that the central Tower Room now displayed new books in the classical Greek collections. However, today Hobbs wasn't interested in anything those collections had to offer; his interest lay solely in a rare text which could confirm the location of a hoard of treasure.

Hobbs did not want the treasure for himself. Rather, he was afraid the treasure would fall into the wrong hands. Small portions of the treasure had already been found, but the majority of it had never been discovered. It could fund the terrorist activities of some small countries and even the nefarious activities of world powers. He shuddered at the thought.

Hobbs took a few steps and then stopped again. This time, he couldn't hear any footsteps. Maybe he had been wrong. It was early evening and people were sure to be around, despite the fact he hadn't seen anyone in this particular section of the reading room. Maybe someone had simply paused to look at a book. Having managed to assure himself he was safe, he pushed on.

The sixth century B.C. King Croesus of Lydia was famous for his untold wealth. After all, that's where the expression 'As rich as Croesus' had come from. Hobbs knew Croesus had funded many public projects and had been generous to the Greeks.

It was only by coincidence Hobbs had stumbled across an ostracon that mentioned the copper scroll. The broken piece of pottery stated that a copper scroll held the whereabouts of the main repository of Croesus's treasure.

Copper scrolls were uncommon. There was the

famous one, 3Q15, one of the Dead Sea Scrolls discovered in 1952 at Qumran. That scroll too was a list of treasure, of sixty-four locations along with an inventory of treasures in each location. If that treasure were to be found today, it would be worth billions. That scroll was dated some six hundred years after the Croesus copper scroll, but one thing was certain, the treasure of Croesus would be worth billions also. Hobbs had to stop the scroll from falling into the wrong hands.

It was only when an old friend of his, Dr. Abigail Spencer, had invited him to give a paper at the Conference of Iron Age Anatolia in celebration of the release of the Lydian Dictionary Project, that he remembered the ostracon. At the time, he had only translated the first part, which told of the fall of the Lydian Empire and the dispersal of the treasure.

After he published an article on the ostracon, a man from Ephesus had contacted him to say he had a copper scroll mentioning the Croesus treasure. He said he wanted to protect the treasure and asked Hobbs not to publish further on the matter. At first, Hobbs thought the man was a fraud, and had not bothered to reply to his email.

After Abigail got in touch, Hobbs translated the

whole shard of pottery. He had no wish to give a paper at the conference but thought his research would help Abigail.

As soon as he finished translating, he knew he had to uncover more information. The ostracon mentioned a copper scroll listing the locations of the treasures. He had emailed the man from Ephesus back, and the man had told him the copper scroll did not, in fact, mention all the treasure. He said it was broken.

This struck Hobbs as true, because he knew the 3Q15 scroll was broken into two pieces when discovered. The man told Hobbs the ostracon was likely a copy of an earlier inscription which detailed the treasure in full. He said he had no idea of the inscription's classification or location.

Hobbs had tried to find out the man's interest in the matter, and had failed convincingly. Still Hobbs, by a fortunate coincidence, was sure he knew the very inscription.

Hardly any Lydian inscriptions survived, just over a hundred, and most were fragmentary. However, Hobbs's doctorate had been on Hipponax of Ephesus, an ancient poet who spoke Lydian. He knew the very volume he needed: a single volume containing Greek translations of sixth century

Lydian ostraca in the Bayriver Collection. These were earlier translations made before the last few decades' significant advances in word meaning. He wasn't a lexicographer and so he wanted Abigail's opinion on this.

Despite the fact the volume was the only one in existence, it was on the shelves.

Hobbs stopped and looked around the library. For a moment, he stood still, struck by its beauty and grandeur.

There was the footfall again—he forced himself to hurry on.

Hobbs spotted the volume he needed but was sure he was being followed. He didn't want to lead anyone to it, so he skirted around and pulled another book from the shelf, one of Ammonius's commentaries on Aristotle.

He pretended to read it and then put it back. He then went back to look for the volume he needed, made a mental note of where it was, and walked straight past it. He continued to another bookshelf in the nineteenth-century section and selected a rare book, a Greek patristic text from the library of Dr. Robert Holmes.

Hobbs sat at the long table and pretended to study the book. If the man from Ephesus had set him up and someone was following him, then he would be sure to lead them to the wrong book.

Hobbs leaned over the book. He took off his gold-rimmed, tortoiseshell reading glasses, polished them on his plain white shirt, and popped them back on the end of his nose.

The footsteps were closer now. Hobbs looked up into the face of a man. This man did not look as though he were either a student or member of the academic staff. He looked more like a mercenary, a trained killer. Hobbs shook himself to dispel such foolish thoughts.

He smiled at the man who was looking straight at him. The man afforded him a slight nod. The man had an aquiline nose and high cheekbones. Hobbs idly thought he looked like the image of Scipio Aemilianus, the Roman Emperor. The man walked over and selected a book and sat down at a nearby table to read it.

The hair stood up on the back of Hobbs's neck. He didn't think this man was a scholar. He didn't have that slightly worn look about him, nor did he show any excitement at reading a rare book.

Hobbs stood up, put the book back on the shelf, and walked away briskly.

As he did so, he heard footsteps. He looked

around to see the man reaching for the Greek patristic text he had just put back on the shelf.

The man saw him watching and ran at him. Hobbs took off at a sprint. He had played football in college and occasionally went for a jog, but he was in no fit shape for running. As he ran, he thought about pulling books off the shelves to delay his attacker, but he couldn't bring himself to harm a rare book.

Hobbs ran ever faster, all the while painfully aware of the footsteps closing on him.

He rounded the corner, but the man had beaten him to the exit. Hobbs turned around and ran back the way he came. He tried to call for help, but he was running too fast to manage a shout.

Hobbs rounded a corner and ran straight into the man's stony chest.

The man pulled a knife on Hobbs, but just as the tip reached Hobbs's body, someone called out. The man swung away as he drove the knife in.

His attacker took off, leaving Hobbs dying on the ground.

Hobbs looked up into the face of a young student bending over him. "Tell her Revelation two, verse two."

Those were his last words.

3

PENNSYLVANIA

DR. ABIGAIL SPENCER PAUSED AS SOME latecomers arrived. She let out a long sigh. Abigail's hours had been cut to part time, and her under-qualified colleague, Dr. Harvey Hamilton, had been promoted over her simply as he was having an affair with the Dean, a woman who doted on his every move. Money would have been tight for Abigail if it hadn't been for the retainer paid to her by a covert government organization.

Abigail had recently been captured by agents of Vortex, a sinister group, but had managed to escape with a government agent, Jack Riley. After Riley recruited her, she hadn't heard another word from him. At least the money kept coming on a weekly basis.

Abigail looked up and saw that everyone was seated. She gestured to the screen once more. "And of course, to this day, no one has discovered what really happened to Croesus," she said. "According to Herodotus..."

A male student in the front row interrupted her. "What about the treasure?"

Abigail pulled an expression of distaste. "Treasure!" she said with disgust. "That's why the Egyptian civilization is so well-known at the expense of several other civilizations such as the Hittites."

She noted some of the students exchanged glances. They'd been on the receiving end of her displeasure over treasure before.

"Has the Croesus treasure ever been found?" the young man persisted.

Abigail nodded and then shook her head. "No, only in part. In 2006, it was discovered that two artifacts from Croesus's treasure had been stolen from a Turkish museum and replaced by fakes. One was a hippocamp and one was a golden bird. They were eventually returned."

"What's a hippocamp?" the same student asked. His question was met with groans.

"A winged horse sea creature," the student sitting next to him said.

Abigail pushed on. "These were part of the treasure known as the Lydian Hoard or the Karun. There were three hundred and sixty-three Lydian artifacts."

"But there would have been much more Lydian treasure than that. Why wasn't *all* the treasure found?" someone asked her.

She shrugged one shoulder. "It's very rare that a whole stash of ancient treasure is found at once. Take Tutankhamen, for example."

She would have said more, but someone called out, "The curse!"

Abigail resisted rolling her eyes. If there was one thing the students liked more than treasure, it was curses.

Just then, she looked up as someone else entered. She pointedly looked at her watch and up again. To her surprise, it wasn't a student, but Jack Riley.

She stared at him fixedly. Some of the other

students turned around to look. Instead of taking a seat, he continued down to her and bent close to her ear. "You have to come with me now." His tone was insistent.

She made to object, but his hand was already on her elbow, leading her out a side door, giving her barely enough time to reach for her jacket. "What's this about?" she asked him.

"I'll explain when it's safe," he said.

She gestured behind her. "But the students! What will they think?"

Riley did not respond. He was looking around and guiding her through the corridors at speed. "We have a mission."

"A mission?" Abigail parroted. She could hardly believe her ears. Could the timing be any worse? "But I have to give a paper at an important conference next week," she protested. "I haven't heard anything from you for weeks and now you turn up and say there's a mission?"

Riley stopped his long strides to turn to her. "Your life could be in danger. Have you heard from Professor Hobbs lately?"

Then he was off again, leading her along. Abigail was entirely confused. "Jason? What's this got to do with him?"

"He was murdered a few hours ago in Oxford."

Abigail was aware her mouth had fallen open. She grabbed Riley's arm. "England? He was murdered? What was he doing in Oxford?"

"I was hoping you could tell me."

Riley guided Abigail to the left. "Why are we going this way?" she asked.

"In case someone is waiting out the front for us." Riley's reply was curt.

Abigail had no doubt a gun was inside his jacket. Abigail knew nothing about guns. Her knowledge only extended to ancient languages and ancient lands. They didn't have guns in her area of expertise. Sure, she knew the difference between a Thracian broadsword and the hoplites' short sword, the *xiphos*, knowledge that would be of absolutely no help in her current predicament. Moments ago, she didn't even know she *had* a predicament.

They reached the side door. She saw a black car with tinted windows outside. "Wait here," Riley said. He looked out the door and then stepped outside, still looking around. He opened the door to the black car. "Get in as fast as you can."

As soon as Abigail stepped into the daylight, bees whizzed past her. It took her a moment or two to realize they were bullets. The next thing she knew, Riley was half pulling, half pushing her inside the car. He jumped in behind her, slamming the door. "Get down," he said as he sped off.

Abigail didn't need telling twice. She stayed on the floor as the car swung this way and that. After the car straightened up and accelerated, she said, "Is it safe to get up now?"

"Sure," Riley said. "It's a bullet-proof car."

Abigail wondered why he had told her to stay down. She was still trying to take it all in. It was all so surreal. "What's this all about?" she asked for a second time.

"It's all about the Croesus treasure," Riley told her. "There is apparently a copper scroll that gives its location."

Abigail scratched her head. She was going to ask a question, but Riley pushed on. "Apparently, the treasure was dispersed and hidden in several locations."

Abigail nodded slowly. "Jason Hobbs recently published a paper on an ostracon that stated that, although there's believed to be a repository of the main treasure. Anyway, please go on. What happened to Jason?"

"Someone from Ephesus contacted him purporting to have a copper scroll which gave the location of one of the stashes of the Croesus treasure. Hobbs went to the Bodleian library."

"What was he looking for?" Abigail said.

Riley shot a look at her. "I was hoping you could tell me."

She wished he would keep his eyes on the road, driving at such speed. "I don't have a clue. You'll have to tell me more."

"We don't know. This has all just happened. We were only alerted to it because we had someone tailing one of Vortex's men."

Abigail caught her breath. She knew the mysterious organization, Vortex, employed mercenaries who would stop at nothing to get what they wanted.

Riley was still talking. "Our man was waiting outside the Bodleian Library when word came that someone was dead. When we discovered it was Professor Hobbs, we wondered what he had that Vortex would want. We went through his phone records and email exchanges and discovered he'd been corresponding with a man from Selcuk about the copper scroll."

"Selcuk? That's right next to the ruins of ancient Ephesus."

Riley nodded. "The man told Hobbs there was an earlier translation of the copper scroll."

Abigail tapped her forehead. "Of course! Hobbs did send me an offprint of his most recent article on the ostracon."

Riley shot a look at her again. "I'm hoping you can explain his dying words."

Abigail was still upset over the loss of her former colleague and friend. "What were his words?"

"He said, 'Tell her, Revelation two, verse two.' Do you have any idea what that means?"

Abigail didn't have a chance to respond, as a car pulled up beside them and slammed into them.

4

EPHESUS

Eymen Bulut wasn't a paranoid man. At least, he hadn't been until now. A respectable jeweler, Eymen had gone about his life in obscurity. Decades ago, Eymen's father had let him in on the secret of the copper scroll.

His father had issued the dire warning that the scroll must not fall into the wrong hands. Eymen's father had died in a car accident only weeks after Eymen's sixteenth birthday, on which occasion he told him the whereabouts of the scroll and promised to tell him more about it later. Now, at the age of forty-seven, the burden still lay heavily on Eymen.

For years, Eymen had kept an eye on all the relevant academic journals, the *Journal of Near Eastern Studies*, *Anatolian Studies on JSTOR*, *Belleten*, the *Journal of Greek Archaeology*, and other journals that mentioned Lydia, searching for any mention of the Croesus treasure. He had read every report, monograph, and article published by Harvard's *The Sardis Expedition*. When he read Professor Hobbs's paper, he had tentatively reached out to him.

From their correspondence, Eymen became certain that Hobbs was not after the money.

Still, their latest correspondence had been different somehow, and Eymen wondered if someone was intercepting their emails.

And so it was with great trepidation he caught a bus to the ruins at Ephesus to meet with Professor Jason Hobbs.

Eymen wanted to speak with Hobbs in person. He considered himself a good judge of character. Hobbs wanted to go to Eymen's apartment or jewelry store, but Eymen had refused, saying he would meet him at Ephesus. It was only a thirty-minute walk away, but Eymen wasn't taking any chances. That is why he took the bus.

Eymen walked through the ruins of Ephesus as he had done many times before. He had grown up in Selcuk, but no matter how many times he visited the ruins of Ephesus, the fact he was walking over the same ground people thousands of years ago had walked still filled him with awe.

He had told Hobbs to meet him in the Bouleuterian. It was a fitting place as it was where city matters were discussed in ancient Ephesus. Theatrical performances were also held there.

Eymen walked behind the Basilica Stoa and into the Prytaneum. The crowds weren't as prolific as usual, given it was late winter and thus not the tourist season. A pang of anxiety hit him. What if Hobbs was simply there to procure the scroll and wanted the treasure for himself?

Eymen had been consumed with misgivings before. Now it was too late. He would have to push forward and meet the man.

Eymen took a firm hold on the handle of his leather briefcase and looked around for Hobbs.

His eyes fell on a tall man. He had a slightly stooped, wearied expression and was wearing a tweed coat. Surely, this was the academic he was supposed to meet.

The man caught his eye and smiled and waved.

He walked over to him. "Eymen Bulut?" the man said, offering his hand.

Eymen nodded. "And you must be Professor Hobbs."

The man shot him a good-natured smile. "Call me Jason."

All the hair stood up on the back of Eymen's neck. The man was an academic—he expected him to have soft hands. These hands were hard and calloused. Eymen looked down to see the man's fingernails were stained. These were not the hands of a person who spent his life indoors. He looked up into Hobbs's face. He would have expected a pale face, but the man's face was tan with deep lines, signifying he had spent much of his time in the sun. Even the loose jacket was unable to hide the bulging biceps.

Realization hit Eymen like a ton of bricks. This was not Professor Hobbs.

Without further word, he sprinted up the steps from the bottom of the Bouleuterian.

Another man appeared at the top of the steps and made to block his way. Eymen took advantage of the group of tourists that appeared, veering around them and sprinting for the Prytaneum. He knew his way around the boulders.

Eymen wanted to run in the other direction, but he risked a glance over his shoulder and saw five men now following him. He had to stick with the tourists. He had no doubt the men would shoot him if he ran for the solitude of the rocky hills. Right now, he thought he would be safe so long as they didn't lay hands on him. He deftly ducked around the boulders of the Prytaneum and headed for the Pollio Fountain in the Temple of Domitian. The scaffolding was still over the Pollio Fountain, but that was of no help to him.

His breath was coming in rapid bursts, but at least he was heading downhill from the top to the bottom of Ephesus. As he approached the ancient Curetes Street, he ducked behind the sculptured figures on the columns of the Memmius Monument to catch his breath. There were no tourists here.

Eymen had no idea what he could do. A rudimentary plan to save himself took form in his terrified mind. He sprinted away, heading for the Hercules Gate. The glare from the sun momentarily blinded him, but he knew his way.

Eymen figured if he left the briefcase, they might leave him alone. He ran past the two pillars on which were carvings of Hercules. He took a deep breath and flung the briefcase high in the air so his pursuers would see it. Eymen then took off at a straight sprint down Curetes Street, taking care not to trip over the paving stones. It wasn't until he reached the Fountain of Trajan that he ducked behind one of the columns and peeked out. He could have cried with relief when he saw the five men crowding around the briefcase.

Maybe they wouldn't chase him now. They had what they wanted, but Eymen wasn't prepared to take the chance. He looked up at the hill and the sparse bushes behind the Fountain of Trajan. No, he needed to stay closer to people, and the bushes didn't afford any cover. He took off at a fast walk toward the Temple of Hadrian, figuring if he walked rather than ran he would be less noticeable.

Eymen knew he had to find a hiding place, and quickly. Just behind the Temple of Hadrian was a mosaic footpath that led to the terrace houses at Ephesus. He had been in there before, although they had opened to the public only a few years earlier. He paid the fee and slipped inside. Today, he did not look at the beauty of the original paintwork or at the writing etched on the walls. He passed the ancient shopping lists and the prices of vegetables and meat scrawled on the walls and headed down to the living quarters. There, he sat on a magnificent floor mosaic surrounded by frescoes and clutched his arms around himself.

Eymen reached for the phone in his pocket, but it must have fallen out. He shut his eyes tightly and wrapped his arms around his knees, willing the men not to find him. Maybe he should go back and ask someone to call the police for him. Still, he was reluctant to bring the police into it. The police would ask him why the men were chasing him, and the copper scroll had to be kept secret. He could no longer trust anyone. He had trusted Professor Hobbs, but this man was not Hobbs. For all he knew, Hobbs was already dead.

Eymen heard a sound and looked up.

There, framed by modern scaffolding and incongruous against the intact mosaics in their original setting, was a man. The man was pointing a gun at him.

Eymen wondered why the gun was so thick and then realized it had a silencer.

A shot rang out, but Eymen didn't hear it.

5

PENNSYLVANIA

ABIGAIL CLUNG TO THE SIDES OF THE SEAT AS THE dark SUV rammed them again. She shut her eyes tightly. Abigail's head collided hard with the window as Riley swung the wheel to the left. "Sorry about that," he said. She opened her eyes to see a blur of the landscape whizzing past. A wave of nausea hit her.

Abigail was flung this way and that as the car skidded and then swung. Abigail realized they were heading away from the town, away from the safety of people, and wondered if that was a good idea. Still, Riley knew what he was doing.

They passed a phone shanty, used by Amish people to make calls. Abigail knew the road they were on bypassed an Amish community. She hoped they wouldn't pass any Amish buggies, as their speed would surely frighten the horses.

When Abigail risked a look back, she saw they had gained some ground over the pursuing SUV.

When they reached the outskirts of town, Riley turned hard down a dirt road, kicking up a trail of dust. Once more, Abigail wondered about the wisdom of such a plan, as the trail of dust would be visible for miles.

Riley suddenly swung the car to the left. The car bounced along down to a creek until he brought the car to a sudden stop. "Stay down and keep the doors locked," he barked at Abigail.

She was only too happy to do as he said. After a few moments, she craned her neck and saw Riley running back up toward the road.

Abigail felt awfully vulnerable sitting out there as a decoy despite the fact the car was bulletproofed. If only she were armed, but then again she would not know what to do with the weapon.

It wasn't long before she heard a car roaring toward her. She clutched her throat and shut her eyes tightly. What if Riley didn't come back? She couldn't sit in the car forever. But if Riley didn't come back, that would mean he was hurt—or worse. Tears pricked the corner of her eyes.

There was an exchange of gunfire. Abigail clutched her throat. She planted her hands over her ears and trembled.

It seemed like an age before the gunshots stopped. Abigail looked up in fright as someone banged on the window.

It was Riley. He opened the door and jumped inside. "Are you all right?" he asked, her searching her face.

Abigail did her best to put on a brave front. "Fine," she said. "And you?"

Riley simply nodded. "I didn't expect them to be here so fast."

With that, he sped off. Abigail had been hungry, but now the thought of food made her stomach churn. Her breath was coming in ragged gasps and she tried to slow it. "They won't follow us?"

"No, they won't." His tone was grim.

"Where are we going?"

"Selcuk."

Abigail was incredulous. Surely she hadn't heard him properly. "What? Selcuk? In Turkey?"

Riley nodded. "Yes, we're flying there at once."

"But I don't have my passport."

"Don't worry about it."

Abigail regarded him with narrowed eyes. Had the government given her another identity for this mission? And on the subject of missions... Abigail looked over at Riley. "What's the mission?"

"You will be briefed on the plane. Try to relax as best you can."

Relax? Was he mad? Abigail shook her head. Clearly, Riley was used to such goings-on, but she certainly wasn't. The one and only adventure she'd ever had in her life was when agents who were working against both the government and against Vortex had captured her. They had tried to force her to solve a puzzle in an attempt to retrieve the stones on the ancient High Priest's breastplate hidden in a cave in Greece for centuries. It had almost cost her life, and Riley's life for that matter. When Riley had said the government wanted her to work for them, she had thought it would be simply translation work from then on. She shook her head at herself in disgust.

Riley drove at a high speed out of town for over

an hour until they came to a military airport. He gave his credentials to the guard and was ushered in immediately. For some reason, Abigail had thought they would be flying in a passenger jet. She certainly had a lot to learn about covert operations. In fact, her own naïveté was beginning to worry her.

Riley drove the car directly to a black plane sitting on the runway. The two men standing by the stairs stared at Abigail as if she was some type of rarity, making her uncomfortable. They didn't say a word, merely stood back for Abigail to board and then closed in behind her. It was most unnerving.

When Abigail walked inside the plane, she was surprised to see it wasn't as she imagined. Instead of rows of seats on either side, two chairs faced another set of two chairs and a polished burr walnut table sat between them. The chairs were armchairs rather than the usual airplane fare. To the left, was a long table either of walnut or mahogany. Abigail didn't know much about timbers, apart from the fact that the ancient Macedonian sarissas, the long heavy spears introduced by Phillip of Macedon, were made of cornel wood.

Riley indicated Abigail should sit in the window

seat. He sat next to her and buckled his seatbelt. She followed suit. The two men sat opposite her. They were studying her, so she took the opportunity to study them.

The one directly in front of her had a hawk-like appearance. He was tall and slim and looked at her with narrowed eyes and pursed lips. The man sitting opposite Riley had a boyish look about him. He had a round face and twinkling blue eyes. He offered Abigail an easy smile, while the other man simply grimaced. Abigail wondered if they were going to sit in silence the entire trip to Selcuk, or wherever the plane would land. She had no idea of airports in the vicinity.

It wasn't until they were off the ground and ascending that Riley spoke. "We were under fire at the college and we lost them, but then they came after us. I took care of them."

Both men nodded knowingly. "Abigail, this is Ellis and Thatcher. Guys, this is Dr. Abigail Spencer."

"Call me Abigail," she said, wondering if those names were Christian names or surnames.

Thatcher smiled at her, but Ellis narrowed his eyes. Abigail thought perhaps he objected to her presence.

"So can you tell me what this is about?" Abigail finally asked.

Riley nodded. "Professor Jason Hobbs was corresponding with a man from Selcuk by the name of Eymen Bulut, a jeweler. He's lived in Selcuk all his life. He corresponded with Hobbs saying he had a copper scroll, handed down to him by his father. The scroll mentioned the location of the Croesus treasure."

Abigail gasped. "You're kidding! But that seems too much of a coincidence. That's what my upcoming paper is about."

Riley waved one hand at her in dismissal. "It's not so much of a coincidence as you think. You are, of course, aware that Hobbs published a paper on the Croesus treasure?" Without waiting for Abigail to respond, he pushed on. "That was the catalyst. Bulut told Hobbs he had been keeping an eye on the journals for any mention of the Croesus treasure because he was protecting the copper scroll."

Abigail interrupted him that point. "So this guy actually has a copper scroll that tells the location of the Croesus treasure?"

"Well, that's what we're going to find out, but it seems so."

"And you need me to translate it or see if it's genuine?"

"Precisely."

"You mentioned Jason Hobbs's dying words?" Abigail winced when she thought of her friend's death.

"Yes, he said, 'Tell her, Revelation Two, Verse Two.'"

"That's a reference to the Bible," Abigail said.

"Obviously," Ellis, the narrowed-eyed man said. Abigail didn't know if he was being sarcastic. "What does it say?" he continued.

"I'd have to look at the passage to be certain."

"I don't happen to have a Bible on me," Ellis said. Now his tone was overtly snarky.

Riley shot the man a look. "We can simply look at an online Bible." He picked up the iPad lying on the table and tapped away at the screen for a few moments before handing it to Abigail. "What does it say? Does this mean anything to you?"

"It's in English," she protested.

"What do you mean?" Riley asked.

"I assume if Jason left a message for me, then it was something to do with the Greek meaning, otherwise he would have just stated what he wanted to say. I mean, since he went to the trouble of leaving a puzzle in his message, surely it wouldn't be something that would be easily seen in an English translation."

"Good point," Ellis said grudgingly. "Riley, can you get the ancient Greek translation up online?"

"Never mind. Let me see what it says." Abigail reached out her hand for the iPad.

She searched quickly and then read aloud.

> *"I know your works, your toil and*
> *your patient endurance, and*
> *how you cannot bear with*
> *those who are evil, but have*
> *tested those who call*
> *themselves apostles and are*
> *not, and found them to be*
> *false."*

After a few minutes, she said, "I'd like to see the Greek." She pulled up the Perseus Online Library and found the Greek in question.

"I think I know what Jason meant," she said urgently. "This isn't good!"

6

EPHESUS

THE SHOOTER LEFT THE BODY SITTING THERE. IT was just on closing time and that worked in his favor. He pulled his jacket around his shoulders and slipped back into the crowd looking like any other tourist.

The others were waiting for him outside, pretending to study travel guides. They hurried in the direction of the northern car park, the tallest man hanging tightly onto the briefcase. He had flung his jacket over it, lest the briefcase attract attention.

"This had better be the right copper scroll," he said through clenched teeth.

The man standing next to him let out a grunt of displeasure. "Of course it's the right one. How many are there? Bulut thought he was meeting Hobbs. He had no reason to be suspicious."

The man hesitated in his stride and turned to the other. His gray eyes were cold, menacing. His very pores exuded danger. "Never underestimate the enemy, Number Five," he said, his tone icy. "That's what will get you killed."

The other man rolled his eyes. He had heard it all before. "Take the worst case scenario and work back from there."

"We'll take the bus to Kusadasi," the leader said. "We can't risk going back to Selcuk. That is, of course, unless this isn't the correct copper scroll."

The other four men exchanged glances.

The timing once more worked for them. They tumbled onto a bus with a group of tourists, the leader making sure he kept the briefcase hidden. If anyone had noticed the victim carrying a briefcase, then the police would question tourists as to whether they had seen anyone else carrying a briefcase. The leader wasn't someone who took chances.

And Vortex wasn't forgiving.

When they got off the bus in the main shopping area in Kusadasi, the leader sent the man he considered rather dim-witted to buy the most nondescript luggage he could find. He and the other three men sat at an outdoor café away from the main street on which was CCTV.

It was getting dark and the café exterior area was not well lit. The man returned faster with the luggage than the leader expected. He set aside his chicken kebab, opened the largest piece of luggage, placed the briefcase inside, and snapped the latches shut. It was only then he allowed himself a small smirk of satisfaction.

The men were following the plan and so far everything was going well, but the leader knew better than to rest on his laurels. He left the other four men at a hotel and moved onto the next one. He paid cash and gave his fake name using an Oxbridge accent he had perfected over the years. He barely glanced around the lobby, only to take in any potential threats and to check the exits. He was certain they hadn't been followed.

The reception area was dark, just how he liked it. He shoved aside two half-dead ivy plants to hand over a wad of lira to the clerk, an impossibly thin man with a cigarette hanging out the side of his mouth.

As soon as the leader entered his hotel room, he locked the door behind him and then searched the room before crossing to the window to look behind the curtain. There was nothing suspicious in the street: pizza restaurants, bars, shops, and people scurrying this way and that.

The hotel could have been any one the leader had stayed in over the years: heavy timber furniture, dark cream walls, and white crumpled linen on the bed.

The room smelled faintly of cheap tobacco and whiskey with an overlay of pine disinfectant. He let himself back out and locked the door before looking for the exits. In long strides he reached the end of the corridor and opened the fire escape door which was at the opposite end to the elevator. The corridor swung to the left, and to the right was a glass door leading to a small concrete balcony. He pushed the doors open and looked outside. A tall brick fence blocked the view from the street and it was only a short drop to the roof of the next-door building. The leader smiled to himself as he strode back along the corridor.

It was only when he was back in his locked room that he made the call.

The leader was eating takeout pizza, when there was a knock on the door.

"Are you in there, Enzo Petros?" the voice said.

That was the code word name, but even still, the leader was suspicious. He popped the last few onion rings from the pizza in his mouth, adjusted his gun which was already neatly concealed, and opened the door carefully.

He recognized the man, Number Nine. With him was another man he didn't recognize.

The leader locked the door behind them. Number Nine wasted no time coming to the point. "You have it?"

The leader opened the briefcase. Number Nine nodded to the other man who pulled his reading glasses from his pocket along with some white gloves. "We shouldn't look at it under these conditions," the man complained as he pulled on the gloves in what seemed to the leader to be an overly fastidious manner. "It could easily fall apart."

"You only have to look at it long enough to verify it's genuine. Anyway, that's not your area of expertise, is it Professor." Number Nine said it as a statement not a question. "You're an interpreter, not an archeologist or a restoration specialist."

"I'm *not* an interpreter," the man snapped. "I'm a translator. One does not *interpret* ancient texts—one *translates* them."

The leader could see Number Nine was angry. Still, he said nothing but sat and watched.

The man bent over the copper scroll and made several exclamations of delight. He took it over to the rudimentary wooden table by the television and placed it there on a linen handkerchief.

"Is it genuine?" the leader asked.

The man was clearly exasperated. "Give me time. I'm only just having a look at it now."

"Well, what does it say?" Number Nine pressed him.

The academic held up one hand, palm outward, to both of them. "Give me a minute, won't you? This is written in classical Greek."

Number Nine's eyes narrowed. "Should it be written in classical Greek? Or Lydian?"

"Croesus was very generous to the Greeks and they were on excellent diplomatic terms. I expected it to be in Lydian, but it makes sense that it's in Greek."

The leader and Number Nine exchanged

glances. Still, the leader didn't share Number Nine's impatience. He figured translating an ancient text would take some time.

Number Nine appeared to have reached the same conclusion. "I'm not asking you to interpret— I mean translate—it all right now, but if you could tell me if it is genuine or not, that would be a big help. Are you able to tell us that now?" Number Nine spoke slowly.

The man nodded. "Probably. It's in better condition than I expected."

The leader didn't like the sound of that. He had an uneasy feeling something was wrong and in all his years as a mercenary, he had learned to rely on his instincts. If he had to lay odds on it, he would bet this copper scroll wasn't genuine. Maybe he had underestimated Bulut, after all.

The academic continued to peer at the tablet. "I need to have a better look at this, but it's not listing any treasure. It seems to be an inventory all right, but it doesn't mention treasure. It mentions firewood, honey, oil, wheat, meat, as well as hides from sacrificial animals."

"Does it mention gold or treasure anywhere at all?" Number Nine asked urgently.

"I'm looking for words for gold, jewelry, or any

precious metals and I can't see a single mention of them. I've only had a quick look, mind you, but it doesn't mention Croesus or Lydia or anything that could be construed as treasure. I'd say this copper scroll has nothing to do with the treasure."

"So it's a fake?" the leader asked.

"No, it's a genuine document," the academic said. "I'm fairly certain of that. The only thing is, it has nothing to do with the Croesus treasure."

Number Nine strode over to the leader who drew himself to his full height. "And this was all he had in his possession?"

The leader pointed to the briefcase. "That's all that was in the briefcase. His wallet wasn't in there, only that copper scroll. There was nothing else in there."

Number Nine walked over to the briefcase and turned it upside down on the bed. Nothing fell out of it. He produced a knife from his pocket and ripped the lining apart. By the time he had finished, the briefcase was in shreds.

Number Nine turned back to the leader. "Bulut definitely thought he was meeting Professor Hobbs, right?"

The leader nodded. "That's right. He thought he was meeting Hobbs."

"So obviously something tipped him off," Number Nine said. "We'll have to go back to his house and search it."

"We can't do that now." The leader nodded to the television screen. The sound was off, but the channel had just flipped to the evening's news. A journalist was interviewing a police officer outside Eymen Bulut's store. "The police will be crawling all over the place tonight," the leader pointed out.

"You need to find the scroll, or…" Number Nine's voice faded away. "You need to find the scroll," he repeated. "And those RHTF agents will be looking for it too."

A look of disgust spread across the leader's face. "You leave them to me."

7

EN ROUTE TO TURKEY
ALTITUDE: 51,000 FEET

"DON'T KEEP US IN SUSPENSE," ELLIS SAID.

Abigail bit her lip. They mightn't understand. Still, she had no choice but to attempt an explanation. "I think Jason was telling us the man isn't to be trusted."

Ellis raised one eyebrow before running his hand through his thin head of hair. "Man?"

"Obviously the man with the copper scroll. Jason was saying he wasn't to be trusted."

"And how do you come to that conclusion?"

Abigail shot Ellis a look. "This verse mentions false apostles. In the Greek, an apostle is someone who was sent out, anybody who was sent out. 'Apostle' itself is a made-up word. Early Bible translators transliterated the Greek word."

"Plain English, please," Ellis said with a sigh.

Abigail thought she *had* been speaking in plain English. "A transliteration is not a translation. As you would know, Greek doesn't have the same characters of the alphabet as English. Most of the letters look entirely different. If you put the Greek word for 'someone sent out' straight into English letters you get 'apostle'. That's what the translators did—they simply put the Greek words into English letters." She waved one hand through the air. "But all that aside, my point is that the Greek word 'apostle' is translated as 'somebody who is sent out'."

Ellis leaned forward. "Are you saying this word in Revelation means an apostle or what?"

She shook her head. "No. Hobbs was a Greek scholar. He was talking about the original Greek language, not the English translation. I'm sure Jason meant that someone who was sent out was someone who can't be trusted. It was his way to tell us that Eymen isn't to be trusted."

Riley too leaned forward, a movement which caused his arm to brush against her shoulder, sending a jolt of electricity through her. "Yes, that makes sense. Hobbs figured that Eymen had tricked him—sent him off on a wild goose chase to the Bodleian Library, so he could be killed."

"But that doesn't make any sense," Ellis countered. "If someone wanted to kill Hobbs, they could simply kill him. They didn't need to kill him in the Bodleian Library, of all places." He uttered a snort of derision.

Riley appeared unperturbed. "Yes, but Professor Hobbs obviously thought the whole thing was a setup. In his dying moments, he didn't trust Bulut. Whether he was right or wrong about that is yet to be determined. We examined the correspondence between them and it did seem as though Eymen Bulut was on the level."

"But Jason didn't think so at the end," Abigail pointed out.

Thatcher spoke for the first time. "This doesn't really change anything except to make us more cautious, and we intended to be cautious to start with."

Abigail thought it over. "You're right. Surely Jason could simply have said not to trust Eymen

Bulut, or if he didn't want to name him, simply said not to trust the man from Ephesus—maybe even said not to trust the man with the scroll. Why did he attempt to obfuscate matters?"

Ellis was still wearing the same irritated expression on his face. "Because he didn't want anyone to know what he was really saying."

"But why choose a verse from Revelation?" Abigail countered. "He was an ancient Greek scholar, specifically the Iron Age. He was not a Biblical scholar. His area of expertise was Herodotus and Homer. He was more interested in Doric and Ionic dialects than Biblical Greek which was some five hundred to six hundred years later. No, I'm sure there's a reason why he quoted Revelation."

"Eymen was particularly interested in the Book of Revelation," Riley said. "His emails to Hobbs mentioned it was of interest to him, particularly as he was so close to Ephesus, which is named as one of the seven churches of Asia in the Bible."

Ellis cleared his throat. "Can I have a word with you, Riley?"

He stood up and walked to the back of the plane, followed by Riley, who looked back over his shoulder. "Coffee, Abigail? Thatcher?"

Both said they would like some coffee. Abigail could see them having what looked to her like a heated argument. Even from the distance, she could see Ellis's face was flushed. He was gesturing in an animated fashion.

She couldn't hear what they were saying, but she was certain Ellis didn't want her on the mission.

On a more practical matter, Abigail wondered if she should have agreed to more coffee. She'd had a rushed day working on her paper for the upcoming conference, while keeping up her lecture schedule. She hadn't eaten much that day and had lived on coffee and sugar. Right now, she was shaking and she didn't know if it was from the situation in which she now found herself or from being over caffeinated—maybe both. She was starving. Her stomach rumbled loudly and she shot a look at Thatcher.

He seemed to think that was an invitation to talk. "So, I suppose I should say welcome to RHTF."

She raised her eyebrows. "RHTF?"

Thatcher looked over his shoulder. Riley and Ellis had ceased their argument and were making coffee, although were still in conversation. "I hope I didn't let the cat out of the bag. But surely you signed some papers?"

Abigail nodded. "Yes, I did."

Thatcher looked immensely relieved. "The name was on the papers. RHTF, Relic Hunters Taskforce."

Abigail felt a bit of a fool. "Oh yes, well, yes. I vaguely remember that now." Truth be told, she did vaguely remember a name but hadn't quite remembered what it was. "So, the four of us are working for RHTF?"

Thatcher nodded again. "Yes, I've read your file, but the intricacies of your field of research escaped me. What exactly do you do again?"

"My research interest is lexicography," she told him. "I'm not sure if you're familiar with lexicography?"

The blank look on his face supplied the answer, so she pushed on. "A lexicon is a dictionary. Lexicography is the work of dictionary meaning. When people first translated ancient documents from ancient languages, not all the meanings were known at the time, so they made educated guesses at some of the words from the context. Centuries later, many inscriptions and papyri were discovered. These contained previously unknown words in a variety of different contexts. These conclusively show what the words mean. To put it in a nutshell, lexicographers search all these occurrences of words and figure out what the words mean."

"Like a puzzle?"

She nodded. "Exactly. So, when the famous Liddell and Scott Greek Lexicon was produced in 1843, they didn't know the meaning of many of the words, so they made educated guesses. Many think that Charles Lutwidge Dodgson, who you would know by his pen name, Lewis Carroll, based Humpty Dumpty on George Liddell. There's a line in *Alice in Wonderland* that says Humpty Dumpty could make a word mean whatever he wanted it to mean."

"Where in *Alice in Wonderland* does it say that?" Thatcher asked.

Abigail quoted the passage.

> *'But "glory" doesn't mean "a nice knock-down argument,"' Alice objected.*
> *'When I use a word,' Humpty Dumpty said in rather a scornful tone, 'it means just*

what I choose it to mean—
neither more nor less.'
'The question is,' said Alice,
'whether you can make words
mean so many different
things.'

Abigail sighed. "Many people think that was Lewis Carroll being disdainful about George Liddell's lexicography. Jason liked to tell his students that story." She sighed again as she thought of poor Jason. She had known him for years. A likeable man, Jason had been a reputable scholar and a friend. She couldn't believe he was dead.

Abigail was still lost with her thoughts when Riley and Ellis returned. Riley placed a large mug of coffee in front of her. She looked into the liquid pool and saw it was dark. That's all she needed— more caffeine, and strong at that. Her stomach growled loudly in protest.

Nevertheless, she sipped the brew and was glad it was sweet. At least she was getting some carbohydrates into her, she thought with a rueful smile.

"I'm afraid we've had news," Ellis said,

although he was addressing Thatcher. "Eymen Bulut is dead."

"Dead?" Abigail repeated in shock.

"Yes, he was shot in the ruins of Ephesus."

Abigail realized her mouth had fallen open and hurried to shut it. "But what about the scroll?" she asked, not wanting to sound uncaring.

Ellis shook his head. "We don't have a clue."

Thatcher tapped himself on the chin. "So the police found his body in the ruins of Ephesus?"

Ellis nodded.

Thatcher pushed on. "Why would he visit there? He's lived nearby all his life. Maybe he thought he was meeting with Hobbs?"

"Well, that's one conclusion we could draw," Riley said. "It does certainly seem as though their email correspondence has been tampered with, as there's no mention of any such meeting. It could be any number of things, but if that's the case and someone was impersonating Hobbs, then they probably have the copper scroll."

Abigail gripped the chair as the plane suddenly banked hard to the left.

8

RHTF HEADQUARTERS: UNDISCLOSED LOCATION
HOURS EARLIER

RILEY WAS NEVER COMFORTABLE IN THE RHTF offices. He far preferred the outdoors, and the only greenery he could now see was the high-tech roof terrace covered by all sorts of exotic plants. To him, it looked more like a scene from *Lost in Space* than a suite of government offices.

He averted his eyes from the glare of the sun pounding through the vast panorama of floor to ceiling glass windows and forced his attention back to the meeting.

Ellis pushed a folder aside and leaned across the table. "I don't like it."

The director folded his arms over his chest as his lips formed a thin line. "What's the problem?"

Riley always thought the director looked like the Smoking Man from *The X-Files*: the physical resemblance, the air of danger. He wasn't someone to cross.

Ellis winced. "The woman has no training."

"Exactly. She's an academic. Her skills are the type we need for this mission," Riley pointed out.

"That's my point." Ellis drummed his fingers on the table, a movement so sudden he nearly knocked over his glass of water. "She's a civilian. She's an academic. She's of no use in combat."

The director narrowed his eyes. "Let's hope it won't come to that. At any rate, she proved her worth on the mission."

Ellis's face flushed. "But she didn't recover the stones."

"Have you forgotten I was with her at the time?" Riley said.

Thatcher spoke up. "I don't understand your objections, Ellis. We *do* need her. We won't have time to take photographs and send them back to her to translate. She needs to be on the spot."

Ellis appeared to be thinking it over. "You're probably right, but I still don't like it."

The director nodded his head. "If you'll both step outside, I need a word with Riley."

Ellis and Thatcher stood, gathered their notes, and walked outside the door. As soon as the door shut, the director came straight to the point. "Riley, we could have a problem."

Riley arched one eyebrow.

The director handed Riley a coin in a plastic bag. "A Lydian coin. Were you aware coins originated in Lydia?" He did not pause to allow Riley to respond. "They were gold, silver, or electrum, which is a naturally-occurring alloy of gold and silver. The coin you have there is of the lion and bull design. It's been appraised as in *Choice About Uncirculated* condition, which is rare for a coin that age. That coin is worth around fifty-eight thousand dollars."

Riley quickly handed the coin back to the director.

The director turned the coin over. "This was found in the tomb of a Lydian princess. In 1966, over one million dollars was paid for twenty pieces of the treasure found in her tomb by tomb robbers. We, of course, procured some other samples."

He paused. "The size of a Lydian coin represented different monetary values. A small coin today in a lesser condition would be worth at least four thousand dollars. You can imagine how much a whole chest of these coins would be worth, and one chest of coins would be but a minuscule fraction of the Croesus treasure."

He stood up, walked to the window, and then sat down again. "If you can't retrieve the treasure, then make sure that nobody else can."

Riley nodded. Those were his usual orders. "You mentioned a problem?"

"I think we have a mole."

Riley turned ice cold. "A mole?" he parroted. "Not in my unit?"

The director's expression did not change. "I have no idea. Just be on your guard."

"Can you tell me any more?" Riley asked.

The director's response was a curt, "No."

Riley leaned back and laced his fingers behind his head. Great! He didn't want to lead Abigail into danger. And if there was a mole, who could it be? Surely not Ellis or Thatcher? And why wouldn't the director give him any more information?

9

TURKEY

Abigail's stomach clenched as the plane sped along the runway. She was relieved they had landed, but she wondered what lay ahead of her. During the last mission, she had been inside a dark, ancient cave and had walked only inches away from certain death in an abyss.

Surely nothing like that would happen again? She was merely going to translate the scroll. Still, she couldn't help but worry. Maybe she should have thought harder before she joined the organization. At the time, she had no idea she would encounter

any more life-threatening situations. And, if she
were to be honest with herself, part of the attraction
of the job was Riley.

Abigail was on full alert as she passed through
customs and then walked through the airport, a
public not military airport this time.

She was surprised how easy it was to transport
guns on international flights. Riley had told her it
was no problem to transport unloaded firearms in a
locked, hard-sided gun case, along with suitably
secured ammunition, as checked baggage. He
simply had to declare the firearms and ammunition
to the airline and go through a couple of easy
procedures.

It wasn't until Abigail saw the sign, *İzmir Adnan
Menderes Havalimanı*, that she realized she was in
Izmir.

Abigail was tense. Despite the air-conditioning
she felt hot all over. She kept her eye on a man who
appeared to be watching her. Was he a Vortex
agent? Did he have a gun? She was about to point
him out to Riley when he was joined by a woman
with young children.

She breathed a sigh of relief and shook her
head. Her imagination was certainly running away
with her.

Abigail left Riley to use the bathroom. She was afraid someone would inject her with a deadly substance, or at least knock her over the head and push her into a stall. When a woman brushed past her, she jumped away in terror.

Abigail forced herself to take several deep breaths. She couldn't continue to imagine an assassin around every corner. She had to get control of her fears.

When she walked out of the bathroom, Riley was waiting for her. He handed her a soda and a bag of potato chips. "We'll get something more substantial as soon as we can," he told her. Abigail shot him a grateful smile. The potato chips were welcome, but she was worried about the sugar content of the soda. She was already on a caffeine and sugar high. Maybe the potato chips would soak up some of it.

Presently Thatcher joined them, but they had to wait longer for Ellis.

"I hired a car," he said by way of greeting. Without further word, he turned on his heel and marched away. The others followed him.

The car was a white Renault. Abigail climbed into the back seat with Riley, who at once told Ellis the address of a pizza place.

Food had never tasted so good to Abigail. She had no idea when she fell asleep, but sleep she did as she awoke with a start when the car came to a sudden stop. She looked around, startled, taking a few moments to realize where she was.

Riley looked across at her. "We've booked rooms here."

He hurried to the car to take the luggage out of the trunk. He handed a plain brown suitcase to Abigail. "That's yours," he said, frowning.

Abigail knew better than to ask questions in a public place, even though she could see no one around. "Thanks," was all she said.

Ellis reached for the bell and pressed it. Over the bell hung a board, which was leaning haphazardly to the left. On the board were painted the words, 'Night Bell.'

Ellis rang the bell a few more times before a surly looking man, short and portly with a shock of white hair, answered the door. His eyes were bloodshot and he looked as though he had awoken from a deep sleep.

"What you want?" he said in English.

"We've booked," Ellis said.

The man merely grunted and moved aside for them to enter.

Abigail shot a cursory look around the lobby. The floor was carpeted in unpleasant shades of red and orange, and two mismatched upholstered chairs were pushed against one wall. Between them was a small table with magazines flung across the surface.

Ellis handed the man some bills. The man looked at the cash and then looked up at Ellis. "Most people pay online," he grunted.

Ellis shrugged. "I tried to, but the Internet connection kept dropping out."

The man handed a key to Abigail and a key to Ellis. "Room numbers are on the keys." He pointed to the ceiling and then disappeared through a door behind the reception desk.

The men exchanged glances. Riley picked up his suitcase as well as Abigail's. "Come on."

Abigail figured that covert operatives probably chose nondescript hotels such as this one. A wave of nausea hit her as she thought that Vortex agents might be in the same hotel. After all, they were mercenaries, and probably all agents thought alike. The idea offered her no comfort.

When they reached Abigail's room, Riley took Abigail's key and said, "Wait here." He switched on the light. The light was dim and Abigail was exhausted.

He disappeared into the room for a few moments. When he returned, he handed Abigail the key. "The three of us are next door." He pointed up the corridor and then pressed a burner phone into Abigail's hands.

"Don't answer the door to anybody, and I mean *anybody*. I'll call you on this phone in the morning. If I don't call, don't open the door even if I identify myself. Do you understand?"

Abigail said that she did. She walked inside and shut the door before locking and barring it.

The room was just as dreary as the rest of the hotel. It seemed to be clean, at least on a rudimentary inspection. There was a bed, two pillows, a desk pushed up against a wall, and through the open door she could see a bathroom. The tiny shower too seemed to be clean. "That's something at least," Abigail said aloud.

Abigail opened the suitcase to see what was in there. She took out the clothes and saw to her surprise they were all her size. How did they know her size? It seemed a little too personal to her. Still, there were various toiletries so she wasn't about to complain.

Abigail must have been more tired than she thought, because she slept soundly and was awoken by an unfamiliar ringtone. She fumbled for the phone, groggy. It had spent the night under her pillow.

"Can you be ready in ten? Packed and ready to go?" Riley asked.

Abigail put on her best *I am already awake* voice. "Yes."

"I'll call you again before I knock."

After five minutes, Abigail was sitting on a chair just inside the door, waiting for Riley to call again.

"I'm coming to your door now," he said. As soon as he knocked, she opened the door. Riley and Thatcher were smiling, but Ellis's face formed a barely veiled scowl. As Abigail followed the three men down the corridor and into the elevator, she mused on the fact that Ellis didn't like her. Maybe he didn't like civilians on a mission, or maybe she reminded him of his ex-wife and their divorce had been nasty. Of course, Abigail had no idea whether Ellis had ever been married but figured there must be a reason for his attitude.

When they were in the car, she asked, "Where are we going?"

"We're going to speak with Eymen Bulut's wife.

Widow," Riley corrected himself. "She's in Selcuk."
To Ellis, he said, "Take the Old Highway."

"Isn't that slower?" Ellis asked.

"Ten to fifteen minutes slower," Riley said, "but
we don't have a toll sticker or transponder."

Abigail figured they didn't want a credit card
record of their route. She wanted to ask more
questions, but she wasn't comfortable with Ellis and
Thatcher. She looked out the window, enjoying the
scenery and intrigued by a massive stone fortress on
a hill just before they reached Selcuk.

Selcuk itself was nestled in the hills, a
picturesque farming town enveloped by historical
structures.

"That's the apartment above that store there,"
Riley said as they drove straight past the store.

"I thought we were going there?" Abigail asked.

"We have to check out the area first," Riley told
her. Abigail felt somewhat foolish. Of course—that
made sense.

Presently, Ellis drove back and parked down the
road a little way.

Thatcher knocked on the store door. There was
no response and Abigail wondered if the widow was
elsewhere. Finally, a woman opened the door a
crack and said, "I'm closed."

The woman's eyes were puffy and red. Abigail's heart went out to her.

"We're here from the government," Thatcher said, flashing his badge. "And this is Dr. Abigail Spencer. She was a long-term, good friend of Professor Jason Hobbs, who I believe was friends with your husband."

The woman at once turned her attention to Abigail. "You knew Professor Hobbs?" she asked urgently.

Abigail nodded. "Yes, we were good friends. I knew him for years."

The woman opened the door rapidly. "Come inside, all of you."

The woman, who introduced herself as Nehir, led them through the little jewelry shop into a back room and then up a flight of stairs into an apartment. She gestured that they should sit on two large couches.

Abigail cast a glance around the apartment. The walls were painted an unusual shade of pink. The heavy curtains were burgundy and hung over lace, effectively blocking most of the light. The living room smelled spicy, of cinnamon and perhaps cumin. Abigail had been cold, but now she removed her jacket.

"Coffee?"

Everyone said they would like coffee. Abigail wondered whether they really did want coffee or whether it was just something they did to put the person they were questioning at ease. At least Abigail knew that she genuinely did want coffee.

The woman served strong black coffee. To Abigail, it tasted like Turkish coffee. Nehir turned to Abigail. "Have you heard from Professor Hobbs?"

Abigail shot a look at Riley. "I'm afraid Hobbs was murdered the other night in England," Riley told her.

Nehir's hand flew to her mouth. "He's dead?"

Riley nodded. "I know this is terribly upsetting for you, but we think it was connected with the murder of your husband."

"But he thought he was going to meet Professor Hobbs," she said.

Riley shook his head. "Professor Hobbs was already dead at that point."

Nehir dabbed at her eyes. "My husband didn't trust people easily," she said. "Do you have any idea who murdered my husband? And Professor Hobbs?"

"There   are   some   covert   international

organizations that search for ancient treasures or even ancient artifacts," Riley said.

Nehir nodded. "Yes, Eymen often said that museums were robbed and the items would end up in the homes of wealthy Americans. Who murdered my husband, do you know?"

"We don't know, but we do know they were after the copper scroll," Riley said.

The woman looked shocked. Abigail noticed she hadn't poured herself any coffee and her hands were trembling in her lap. "You know about the copper scroll?"

Riley set down his coffee cup. "Yes, we want to keep it from falling into the wrong hands. That's why Dr. Spencer is with us. She can verify the scroll. It would be a terrible thing if the scroll ended up in the wrong hands," Riley added.

Nehir appeared to be hesitating. She turned to Abigail. "Did Professor Hobbs tell you about the scroll?"

Abigail had to think fast. She somehow had to gain this woman's trust. "I'm about to present a paper at the Conference of Iron Age Anatolia. Jason had published a paper on an ostracon that mentioned Croesus's treasure. Jason knew I was giving a paper at the conference and was trying to help me get information."

Nehir chewed her lip. A startled look crossed her face and Abigail wondered if she was about to run from the room.

"It looks like one of these terrorist organizations had access to the email correspondence between your husband and Professor Hobbs," Ellis said. "That's no doubt how they managed to lure your husband to meet them at Ephesus with the copper scroll. To clarify, you say he thought he was meeting Professor Hobbs?"

The woman nodded again. "How do I know I can trust you?"

"Why don't you google Dr. Spencer here? You can see she's a legitimate academic and she was a friend of Jason Hobbs."

Abigail suddenly had an idea. "Just a moment!" She pulled her own phone out of her jeans pocket. She pulled up some photos of herself with Jason at a recent conference and handed them to Nehir. "Here I am with Jason, and if you google me, you'll see lots of photos online."

Nehir took the phone from Abigail and stared at the screen for what seemed an age. Finally, she gave Abigail a searching look and then said, "So as the scroll leads to treasure, you don't want it to fall into the wrong hands?"

"Yes," Riley said firmly. "That would be dangerous."

"And what if you had the copper scroll and got the treasure, what would your government do with that? I don't trust any governments. Who do you work for again?"

Thatcher leaned forward and showed her his badge.

"I really don't know if this is fake or not," she said, "but I do believe this woman is who she says she is." She rubbed her eyes and then pulled a tissue out of her pocket and sniffled into it. "I don't know if I'm doing the wrong thing, but my husband is dead." Her shoulders shook and it was a while before she spoke again. When she did, she added, "My husband took a fake copper scroll to the meeting."

Annabel gasped. The men showed no reaction.

"You're sure?"

She nodded vigorously. "He guarded the whereabouts of that scroll all his life. He took the wrong scroll to the meeting."

"How long will it take them to discover it's a fake?" Ellis asked Riley.

"What was on the fake copper scroll?" Abigail asked. "And what language was it?"

Nehir shrugged one shoulder. "Eymen said it was inventory and it was in ancient Greek."

"Inventory of treasure? Or of something else?"

"Perishable goods."

Abigail tapped herself on the head. "Then anyone who can read ancient Greek will know it's not the genuine scroll."

The woman wrung her hands. "That's what I've been afraid of. I thought they'd come back here and try to make me tell them where it is."

"And no one has spoken to you yet?" Riley asked her.

She shook her head. "Only the police. Although it was strange that two sets of police came and I had to repeat the same thing to the second officer."

"I'm going to have you extracted for your own safety," Riley said. "It won't be safe for you to return home until after we find the copper scroll. You're going to be in danger until then. We might find it in a day; we might find it in a week or it might be longer. Are you prepared for that?"

"There's nobody I can turn to now and there's nowhere I can go," she said, trembling once more.

Riley nodded. "You'll be safe. Now tell me where the scroll is."

"I don't have a clue," she said. "My husband hid it."

Thatcher leaned forward. "In this apartment? In the jewelry store?"

She waved her right hand through the air. "I have no idea, but he left a clue."

"What is it?" Ellis was clearly doing his best to remain patient.

"I'll get it for you," she said. She crossed to the window and opened the curtains before leaving the room. Riley jumped up and went with her. She returned with an old, leather-bound Bible, which she set down on the coffee table. From it, she pulled out a piece of notepaper. She handed it to Riley.

He read it and then handed it to Abigail.

10

SELCUK

"They've been in there a long time," the blonde man said. "The wife is probably telling them where the real scroll is."

The leader gave a nod of affirmation. "I'm sure she is." He would soon know—the Intel would come through. He had eyes on the group and no one else but him knew this. He knew their every move. Aloud he said, "We'll follow them and we need to make sure we stay out of sight. They'll lead us to the copper scroll."

"But won't they know we're going to do that?"

"They won't know for certain unless they see us, will they?" He shot the man a hard look.

The man flinched and looked away. The leader was still seething about Eymen Bulut leading them astray. Who would have thought he would have the foresight to swap the copper scroll? And how many of those things were there? The leader had been given to understand copper scrolls were uncommon in ancient times. His eye twitched as he fought to quell the anger that so often consumed him.

"There." The blonde man nudged him.

He looked through the scope. There was the academic they were dragging along with them and there were the RHTF agents, Riley, Thatcher, and Ellis. He scowled.

He was so lost in thought it took him a moment to realize the man was still speaking.

"Why don't we just abduct the woman and force her to take us to the scroll? We could take out the other agents."

The leader shook his head in disgust. He would have to keep an eye on this agent. He could prove to be trouble. "Those aren't my orders. You are to follow my orders. Understand?"

This time the man met his gaze, but he nodded.

"If our orders change, then you'll be the first to know."

"Why don't we force the widow to tell us what she's no doubt telling them?"

A muscle ticked in the leader's jaw. "Because we want them to lead us to the scroll. If they hear anything has happened to the widow, they will take extra precautions, and we don't want that."

The man turned to look through the scope. "They're standing up. They must be leaving. Shouldn't we hurry?"

The leader shook his head. "I'll know soon enough where they're going."

"What? You have a tracking device on them?"

The leader smirked. "Something like that."

"What if there's a back way out of there?" one of the men asked him.

"And that's exactly why we have someone watching the back entrance onto the street," the leader said. These men irritated him. Still, Vortex paid him highly. And if Vortex wanted these men to tag along with him, so be it. So long as they didn't get in his way.

The blonde man looked up. "They're coming out."

"Let's hurry," the leader said.

They stashed their gear back in their suitcases and walked down the stairs from the room they had rented to keep an eye on Bulut's store and apartment. There were two hotels on that road, both offering a view of the store. One of the rooms with a view over the street had been vacant, but even if it hadn't been vacant, the leader would have found a way to make it vacant.

The man slid into the street, and then the leader himself took the wheel.

"I'm the driver," one of the men protested.

"Not for now," the leader said as another man slid into the back seat. "Did you get that tracking device on the car?" the leader asked him.

"Yes."

"I'll stay far enough back so they don't see us."

"What's the plan?" the man asked. "Did you see anything?"

The leader shrugged one musclebound shoulder. "The curtains were shut most of the time. For now, we'll follow them."

"Maybe they have the scroll in their possession," the man continued. "Should we ambush them?"

The leader took one hand off the wheel to rub his forehead. He would have to complain about these men. Surely Vortex could have found better men than these. Pack of idiots!

"No, because we don't know if they have the scroll for sure," he said with forced patience. "And no one shoots unless on my orders. Understood?"

The men all answered in the affirmative, and quickly.

"I'll know soon enough if they have the scroll. But for now, we'll follow them at a distance."

The leader gripped the wheel with both hands. It did look as though the RHTF agents were heading back to the airport. If they had the scroll, then they would go to the airport. The only other reason they would go to the airport was that Eymen had hidden the scroll far away. But why would he do such a thing? Surely there were plenty of good hiding places around Selcuk to hide the scroll. It didn't make sense.

No, it looked to him as though they did have the scroll in their possession. And then he would have to arrange an accident for the group.

First, he would wait for confirmation.

11

SELCUK

"WHAT IS IT?" THATCHER ASKED AS SOON AS they were in the car.

They had gone out the back door, through some alleys, and found their way to the car. Anyone watching the store entrance would not know they'd left. They had waited until a man and a woman had materialized out of nowhere and escorted the widow out the back door.

The agents had arrived soon after Riley made a call. Abigail realized they had been nearby the whole time. She noticed that Ellis and Thatcher both looked irritated, no doubt as they too had been unaware of the other agents' presence.

Before Abigail could speak, Riley said to Ellis, "Head back to Izmir while we figure this out." He nodded to Abigail to proceed.

"It's a quote, two verses in Revelation Chapter Two," Abigail said. "The note quoted an English translation:

> *And to the angel of the church in*
> *Pergamon write: 'The words*
> *of him who has the sharp*
> *two-edged sword.*
> *I know where you live, where*
> *Satan's throne is.'"*

"It doesn't mean a thing!" Ellis snapped.

Abigail took a deep breath and pushed on. "And there's more. He wrote 'Revelation 3:18' under it, but he didn't quote that verse."

Riley turned to Abigail and lifted one eyebrow. "Abigail, is Satan's throne a reference to a specific location?"

"Satan's throne is likely a reference to the Altar of Zeus. The podium is still in Pergamon today, but the altar is in the Pergamon Museum."

"So we head to Pergamon?" Thatcher asked.

Abigail shook her head. "The Pergamon Museum is in Berlin."

Ellis grunted. "Could it mean anything else?"

Abigail thought for a moment. "Pergamon was the cult center of Asclepius, the Greek god of healing. The Greeks described him as a mighty miracle worker. Still, a reference to Asclepius would be too obscure in the context. The consensus among Biblical scholars is that the throne of Satan is a reference to the Altar of Zeus, so it would make sense that Bulut followed this line of reasoning."

"Surely Bulut didn't hide the scroll in a museum in Berlin," Ellis continued in more reasonable tones, "and it seems just as unlikely that he dug a hole under the podium in Pergamon and buried it there. The note may be a clue, but it's not an obvious clue. So do we go to Pergamon or Berlin?"

"We can't go to Berlin," Abigail said. "The Pergamon Exhibit has been closed for years and won't be opened for a few more years yet."

"And it doesn't make sense to go to Pergamon," Riley agreed, "at least not yet. Abigail, tell us everything you know about the Altar of Zeus."

Why is it so hard? Abigail thought. *The clue should*

surely be more obvious than this. Aloud she said, "We're forgetting the other clue: Revelation 13:18."

Riley was already searching on his phone before Abigail finished talking. He read the verse aloud.

> *"'This calls for wisdom: let the one who has understanding calculate the number of the beast, for it is the number of a man, and his number is 666.'"*

He turned to Abigail. "Does that make sense?"

Abigail nodded slowly. "There are some nuances in the original Greek, but all that aside, I think this clue refers to a person. The two Scriptures have to be linked."

Ellis made a strangled sound at the back of his throat. "A Satanist? You want us to look for a Satanist?"

"Of course not!" Abigail said. "I'm just saying that the second clue suggests it's a person."

Thatcher piped up. "Or maybe the clue is the number 666? An address in Pergamon?"

"Pergamon is now Pergamum. The Pergamon of the Book of Revelation is no longer standing,"

Abigail told him. "It's all ancient ruins now. Possibly the clue *is* to a street number, 666, but that would be too obvious."

Ellis snorted, drawing Riley's ire.

"Drop the attitude, Ellis!" he said firmly. "Can *you* do any better? If you have a theory, maybe you should speak up now."

Abigail shot Riley a grateful look. It was hard to concentrate under circumstances such as these and Ellis's continual attitude certainly did not help matters. She considered for a moment before speaking. "Maybe there are two clues in Revelation Chapter Two: the sword and the Altar of Zeus. Riley, can I have that iPad?"

"I don't know if this is it, but it certainly fits," she said after several minutes. "There's a knife shop in Pergamon Street, Selcuk. The name of the knife shop is *Pergamon Blades*."

No one spoke for a moment. Abigail thought she had better say something else. "What if we are meant to contact a person rather than find a buried clue or read an inscription or the like? Nehir said the copper scroll had been in the family for centuries. It stands to reason that more than one person would be entrusted to protect it."

Thatcher craned his neck in the passenger seat

and turned to look at Abigail. "You mean like a secret society? A secret society entrusted with keeping the copper scroll safe?"

Abigail shrugged. "I don't know about a secret society as such; I was thinking more of a group of men entrusted to guard the scroll. Maybe the scroll is being hidden by someone in the *Pergamon Blades* knife shop."

This time Riley was quick to speak. "It does make sense," he said. "If Eymen knew there was a clue or even the scroll itself in Berlin, he wouldn't have left that piece of paper. As it is, the clues he left do tend to suggest what Abigail is saying. It won't hurt to look. Turn the car around, Ellis."

Abigail was surprised Ellis did not object. After a moment, Riley leaned forward and tapped him on the shoulder. "Actually, drive to the airport. We'll swap cars just in case someone's tracking this one."

"If we go to the knife shop, how do we make the person trust us?" Abigail said. "If his family's been guarding the copper scroll for generations, why would he hand it over now?"

"For the same reason Eymen's widow handed over a clue," Riley said. "Others are on the track of it now, and it can't fall into the wrong hands.

Obviously, Eymen thought they no longer had sufficient resources to guard the scroll."

Abigail's head was spinning. Was she right about that clue? Would it even be worth going to Pergamum and having a look around the Altar of Zeus there? She thought not. What clue could possibly be there? Any graffiti would have been removed by now and people were hardly likely to leave a clue buried under something. No, the more she thought about it, the more she thought she was right.

Her stomach rumbled loudly and she wondered when government agents ever found time to eat.

"We'll eat soon," Riley said to nobody in particular.

Abigail was relieved that Ellis hired a new car quickly, and soon afterward, stopped the car in a busy street filled with cafés.

They all piled out and followed Riley into a modern yet cozy café. The marble floors screamed expense. The walls were rendered white, and the unusually shaped ceiling lights cast shadows reminding Abigail of a spaceship. The chairs were yellow, but a red cloth was draped over the back of each chair.

The menu was in English as well as Turkish.

Abigail was surprised to see it was a pizza restaurant. Nothing else was on the menu, simply pizzas with seafood, all types of meat including smoked tongue—Abigail was going to avoid that one—pizzas with cheese only, pizzas with vegetables, and even sweet pizzas.

Abigail realized they had chosen a table at the back of the room so they could see outside the window. She noticed all three men glanced surreptitiously out the window from time to time and she was certain Riley kept the road outside in his peripheral vision at all times.

The men ate quickly. Abigail was a slow eater, so did her best to eat faster.

As soon as they were back in the car, Riley said, "The knife shop is next to a Turkish delight shop and a spice shop. We'll go into every shop on that street and stay in each one for several minutes, to confuse anyone who's following us."

Ellis cracked his knuckles. "And if Abigail's right and this is the person Bulut wanted us to contact, then he might not have the scroll in his possession. He might simply have another clue."

Abigail had been thinking that, but she hoped it wasn't true. Despite the fact she had always planned to spend time in Turkey, she had planned it to be on vacation and at a leisurely pace, not running around looking for clues leading to an ancient copper scroll with assassins hard on her tail. Her stomach churned and she wished she hadn't eaten so quickly. She reached for the bottle of water at her feet and took a few slow sips.

Soon they were driving down the winding streets of Selcuk with Thatcher navigating. Ellis parked the car outside a rug store and they all got out. Abigail did her best to act like a tourist, staring in every window. The first shop they went into was the spice shop.

It smelled delightful. Abigail almost forgot the real reason she was there and looked at the rows of bottles on wooden shelves.

Abigail turned to look at some pink Turkish tea crystals and did a double-take at a man looking on the shelves by the front window. Was he following them? He looked like a man she had seen at the airport earlier when they were getting a different hire car. She quietly pointed him out to Riley.

"Stay here until I get back," he whispered. His breath was warm against her ear, sending little shivers of electricity down her spine. She did her best to turn her attention to the rows of spices: cardamom, turmeric, and fenugreek.

Before long, Riley was back at her side. "He's a local man," he said.

"I'm sorry."

He patted her back briefly. "Don't be sorry. It's better to be safe than sorry. Just between us, I don't think we've been followed."

"That's good, isn't it?" Abigail said, wondering why Riley didn't sound pleased.

He shook his head ever so slightly. "If we not being followed, it means they know exactly what we're doing."

She was about to ask him to clarify when Ellis walked over to them. "Turkish delight next?"

They walked into the Turkish delight shop which doubled as a little café. "Maybe we should sit here and look over the street at the locals, to take in the local culture," Riley said.

Everyone knew what he meant. They sat down in a booth. Abigail sat next to Riley, who this time had the window seat. Riley ordered for her— Turkish coffee, a small glass of peppermint, and a glass of water as well as some Turkish delight.

"Drink the water first," Riley suggested. "The Turkish coffee is very thick and strong, and the water makes it taste better. It's healthier that way too."

"And the peppermint?"

Riley looked confused. "I have no idea, only that it's traditional to drink it with Turkish coffee, or it was when I first started coming to Turkey. It's thick and sugary."

Abigail had read about this and was keen to try it. The Turkish delight melted in her mouth. It was nothing like the Turkish delight she'd had back home. For a moment, she almost forgot the urgency of her problems. She stared out the window but didn't see anybody suspicious. Then again, what would someone suspicious look like? Agents would be too well trained to look like mercenaries—they would blend with the locals. Maybe she was looking at a Vortex agent right now. She shuddered at the thought.

Soon the pleasant divergence was over and they walked next door into the knife shop. A bell rang as they walked inside. The man behind the counter looked up, seemingly startled to see them.

"Are you the owner?" Riley asked him.

"This store was my great-grandfather's," the man said. "It's been here for years."

"I'm afraid we don't have time to beat about the bush," Riley said. "We've come straight from Eymen Bulut's house."

A look of fear and something else that Abigail could not identify passed across the man's face.

"Eymen's dead," he spat.

"Yes."

Riley nodded to Abigail so she supposed she was to mention Jason. "I'm an academic and Professor Jason Hobbs was a good friend of mine," she told the man. "Eymen Bulut was to meet my friend, Jason, but somebody impersonated him. At the time of the meeting, Jason had already been murdered at the Bodleian Library in Oxford. He was there researching a copper scroll."

The man narrowed his eyes. "The Dead Sea Scrolls."

Abigail knew he was trying to throw them off the track or maybe test her to see what she knew.

She shook her head. "No, not 3Q15. This copper scroll was Lydian." She pulled up the photo of her with Jason Hobbs on her phone once more and showed it to the man.

He took her phone and stared at the image. "I am giving a lecture on Lydia's relations with the Iron Age Greeks next week," she said. "Jason Hobbs was doing some research in the same area. That led him to the copper scroll that told of the treasure of Croesus. I think that's why he was murdered in Oxford."

The man handed her phone back and she immediately searched for the conference website. She handed the phone back to the man. "You can see I am who I say I am. I'm giving that lecture next week. Whoever killed Eymen Bulut impersonated my friend, Jason. We're sure of it. Mr. Bulut thought he was meeting Jason, but Jason had already been murdered in England."

She could not help the tear that formed in the corner of her eye and rolled down her cheek. She saw that the man noticed it too. "And who are these men?" he asked her.

"They're helping me," she said. "We can't let the copper scroll fall into the wrong hands, and mercenaries are already after it. Dangerous mercenaries killed Jason and killed your friend, Eymen. They're after the scroll so they can fund terrorist activities with the treasure."

"And what of Nehir Bulut?"

"We got her to safety," Riley said. "She was in danger from the mercenaries."

The man regarded them with fresh interest. "And are you certain you could keep the scroll safe?" He addressed the question to Abigail.

"I'll guarantee I will do my best to stop it from falling into the wrong hands," she said.

Silence hung in the air for what seemed to Abigail like an age. She wondered if the man believed them.

Finally, he spoke. "Eymen said it was no longer safe for us to keep the scroll," he said. "He did want to give it to Professor Hobbs."

Abigail caught her breath. So she was right after all. "Do you have it?" she asked breathlessly.

"I do not," he said. "I'm just the keeper of a clue, I'm afraid. Maybe this clue will lead you to the scroll itself. Maybe it will lead to another clue."

Abigail could not resist a question. "So are you in some sort of secret society, protecting the scroll?"

The man laughed, but it wasn't a laugh of derision. "No, nothing like that," he said. "You've been watching too many American movies. No, Eymen and I were friends, and I have the next clue, but I don't know where it will lead. This is all I know." As if for emphasis, he added, "Eymen and I knew each other, but we didn't know anyone else who was involved. Eymen had the fake scroll, but I have nothing."

"Do you want our protection too?" Riley said.

"They'll be coming after you. They could come for you today. Maybe even within the hour."

The man shook his head. "I can disappear. Some of my trade is not necessarily legal, if you get my meaning."

Abigail didn't get his meaning, but she wasn't about to comment. "I'll get you what you need," the man said before disappearing through a back door.

After he was gone a few moments, Abigail wondered if he'd slipped outside and made a run for it, but he returned presently. He handed her an envelope.

It was yellowing, and the edges crumbled when Abigail touched it. She carefully removed the yellowed piece of paper inside and read it before groaning aloud. She had thought the last clue difficult, but this one seemed impossible.

12

SELCUK

*'And he will rule them with a rod
of iron, as when earthen pots
are broken in pieces, even as I
myself have received authority
from my Father. And I will
give him the morning star.'*

RILEY TOOK PHOTOS OF THE NOTE WITH HIS phone. Abigail handed it back to the man, but he held up both hands, palms outward.

"No! You take it." With that, he hurried

through a door behind the counter and shut it firmly.

"Back to the car," Riley said.

When they were in the car, Riley instructed Ellis to drive around while they discussed the clue before turning to Abigail. "Any ideas?"

She shook her head. "It's another quote from Revelation, but that's all I can tell you. Oh, apart from the fact it's a message to the church of Thyatira."

"Thyatira!" Ellis spat. "Where on earth is that?"

"It's modern day Akhisar, which is probably a Lydian word meaning 'white castle,'" Abigail told him. "I don't think it's far from here."

"Do you want me to drive there now?" Ellis addressed the question to Riley.

Riley raised one eyebrow at Abigail. "Surely not? We don't have enough to go on."

Abigail agreed. "I'm guessing it's the same type of clue that led us to the man in the knife shop. Here we have iron, clay pots, and a morning star."

"So, if we put them together, that should be the clue," Thatcher said.

Abigail nodded. "Hopefully. Maybe it's referring to another store in Selcuk, one that's been there a long time."

For the next few minutes, Thatcher, Riley, and Abigail googled furiously.

"What about this?" Riley said. "Morning Star Ceramics and Silver Gifts."

"Is that the store name?" Ellis said. "It's quite a mouthful."

"No iron is mentioned, but I suppose silver is a metal."

"It's a bit of a stretch, if you ask me," Thatcher said, twisting around to look back at Riley, "but it's certainly worth checking out. And it's in Selcuk?"

Riley gave a nod of affirmation and directed Ellis to the store. It was away from the main shopping district. They parked the car and had to continue on foot. The area was paved and seemed in worse condition than several ancient archeological sites Abigail had visited. There was a high brick wall topped with gray stone to her left and a low brick wall with a row of houses made of red brick to the right. It was beautifully picturesque, but she wasn't there for the scenery.

They walked past several faded blue doors until Riley nodded. "That must be it there."

The door was shut and the curtains were drawn. "It doesn't look like it's open," Abigail said.

Ellis craned his neck. "There's an apartment

over the shop. Maybe whoever is there is afraid after what happened to Bulut."

They walked over the shop and knocked. "You call out," Riley said to Abigail. "You would sound less threatening."

"What will I say?"

"Tell him you're a friend of Professor Hobbs who was a friend of Eymen Bulut's. Say Nehir Bulut sent you here via the knife shop."

"You want me to say all that?" Abigail said.

Riley nodded. Abigail did as he asked. "Hello? I know you're closed, but I need to speak with you urgently. I'm Abigail Spencer, a professor of ancient languages, and I was a friend of Professor Jason Hobbs, who was corresponding with Eymen Bulut."

She was about to say more when the door opened a crack. A man regarded them suspiciously. His face was tanned and filled with deep wrinkles. He wore a look of distrust on his face.

He looked Abigail up and down. "You translate ancient languages?"

"Yes. Did you know Eymen Bulut? He and I had a mutual friend."

The man did not respond to that, but looked at the other three men. "Who are these people?"

Riley stepped forward and showed him his

identification. "We're from an organization that protects ancient artifacts from falling into the wrong hands," he said.

The man regarded Riley shrewdly. "I've heard of this organization. Come in, quickly." He waved his hand furiously at them. "Were you followed?"

"No," Thatcher said. "We were careful."

It only then occurred to Abigail that she had no clue whether they had been followed, yet she knew Riley, Thatcher, and Ellis would have been watching out the whole time.

The shop was attractively decorated, and filled with pretty jewelry and all sorts of ceramics. It was the type of store Abigail could normally spend hours in. The man ushered them through the store quickly and into a small room to the side. He peeked behind heavy blue curtains over a small window. As the curtains fell aside a little, Abigail saw that the window was covered with iron bars.

He closed the door behind them and locked it. "I know you said you weren't followed, but I can't risk it. We can't be too careful. *I* can't be too careful," he added. "I have security but only for thieves, not for the type of people who are after the scroll. Anyway, please sit."

The walls were whitewashed over rudimentary

brick, and the dark brown couches looked hard, but when Abigail sat in one she sank down further than she expected. She wondered if it was so old that the springs had broken. Riley sat next to her, while Thatcher and Ellis sat on the other couch.

The man himself sat on a wooden chair which was upholstered with a bright pattern, reminding Abigail of a Persian rug.

There was another rug on the floor, an intricate pattern in shades of red. Abigail noted that there was one other door out of the room. She wondered why she was becoming observant all of a sudden, and figured it was the company she was keeping.

The man came straight to the point. "How did you find me?"

He addressed the question to Abigail. She raised one eyebrow at Riley and he gave a little nod, so she proceeded. "I'm giving a paper soon at a conference on Lydia and Greece in the Iron Age, and a friend of mine, Professor Jason Hobbs, had already published a paper on an ostracon that mentioned part of the Croesus treasure. It was fragmentary..."

The man interrupted her. "I know about that. Forgive me. You can call me Berat."

Abigail introduced the other men. They all

nodded to each other.

"Go on," Berat said with a wave of his hand.

"Then we heard that Jason Hobbs was murdered in England and after that, someone impersonated him to draw out Eymen Bulut and take the scroll from him."

"And it was a fake scroll," he said.

Abigail nodded. "And so we followed the trail here."

"Through Murat at the knife shop."

Abigail nodded again, but she was uneasy. The man from the knife shop had said he didn't know anyone involved with the scroll, apart from Eymen.

"And so what are you going to do when you find the copper scroll?" Berat addressed the question to Riley.

"We're going to make certain that the treasure doesn't fall into the wrong hands," Riley said.

Berat narrowed his eyes. "You mean you're going to take it for your government?"

Riley shook his head. "I can assure you it will be kept safe."

The man made a sound of derision. "You can't tell me you will donate it to the Turkish museum." He emitted a harsh laugh.

Riley made to speak, but the man pushed on.

"Our group has made sure this treasure hasn't fallen into the wrong hands. We've been protecting it for generations. It's been where it is for almost three thousand years and it should continue to stay where it is."

"Look, I'm in full agreement with you," Riley said, "but we are under time pressure. Some rather dangerous men are after it. They've already murdered Professor Hobbs and your friend, Eymen Bulut. They will stop at nothing to get the copper scroll and then they'll take every last bit of treasure for themselves."

Ellis spoke up. "In fact, if we found you, then they could find you too."

Berat nodded calmly. "Yes, I was about to leave town and hide out."

"Do you have the copper scroll?" Riley asked him.

"No, but I do hold a clue to its whereabouts." He looked at Abigail. "Can you translate the scroll? Is that what you're doing here?"

"Yes," Abigail said. "I'm going to translate it when we find it."

"You're going to translate it, and then you'll all go and find the treasure. Is that right?"

"That's right," Riley said. "But we're not going

to take the treasure. We just want to make sure those men don't find it."

Abigail rubbed her eyes with one hand. This wasn't going as well as she had hoped. This man obviously had no intention of handing over a clue easily. Besides, when he said he didn't have the scroll, she noticed his eyes flickered. She had the sensation he was lying, but she couldn't be sure.

What if he did have the copper scroll? And what if she was in close proximity to it now? A small thrill of excitement ran through her.

"So, you can read ancient Greek?" Berat asked Abigail.

"Yes, I can. It's one of my main areas of expertise. I can also read some Lydian. Is the scroll in ancient Greek or Lydian? Or is it bilingual?"

The man laughed, a short guttural laugh. "You're trying to trick me. Are you sure you weren't followed?" He walked over to the window to look out before returning to his seat once more. "So, these dangerous men who are trying to steal the treasure—how many of them are there?"

"We have no idea," Riley admitted, "but I'm sure there are more than enough to get the job done. It's essential the copper scroll doesn't fall into their hands."

Berat narrowed his eyes. "If I give you the next clue, you'll follow it to the copper scroll, and then follow the copper scroll to the treasure. You'll make sure these other men don't get it?" Before anyone could respond, he added, "And I suppose they want the treasure to fund terrorist activities?"

"Correct," Riley said.

The man appeared to have made up his mind. "All right, you've convinced me. I'll fetch the next clue. Are you certain you weren't followed?"

Riley assured him that they hadn't been followed, but Berat was already halfway across the room.

Abigail was pleased the man had finally relented. For a moment, she had feared he wasn't going to give them the clue and she wondered what Riley and the others would do in a situation like that.

Abigail saw the man as he opened the door, for a split second wondering why he had something strange on his face.

She only barely registered it was a gas mask as something was thrown into the room. The door slammed shut.

The last thing Abigail remembered was coughing.

SELCUK

RILEY CAME TO HIS SENSES BEFORE THATCHER
and Ellis. His eyes stung and his throat was burning,
but that didn't stop him from getting to his feet and
hurrying over to Ellis. "Berat has taken Abigail."

Ellis looked around groggily while Riley shook
Thatcher awake. Riley tried the back door and then
the side door, but both were locked and the window
had bars on it.

Thatcher aimed a good kick at the side door,
but Riley said, "Not that door. There could be

alarms inside the shop. We should go out the back door."

It took a while before they managed to knock the back door down. It led straight into a storage room. The air was fresh and Riley gulped in deep breaths.

"What do we do now?" Ellis asked him.

"I'm tracking her cell phone. I'll find her location."

Ellis put a restraining hand on Riley's arm. "We should search the place. Maybe he's got some evidence lying around."

"Evidence of what?" Riley said.

"We won't know until we find it." Ellis's tone was boarding on belligerent. "Besides, you shouldn't go running after the woman just because of your, err, emotional involvement. We can always find another translator."

"Not one as highly qualified as her, surely," Thatcher said.

Riley shot Ellis an ice-cold glare. Ellis shifted from one foot to the other and looked away. His comments were subordinate, although if Riley were to be honest, there was more than a modicum of truth in his remarks.

"When we find Abigail, we will find Berat. We

won't need any further information after we question him. We're wasting time. Let's go. Unless you have any other objections, Ellis?"

Ellis shook his head. Riley strode to the car and wasted no time turning on his device to track Abigail's phone. "She's heading north," he said. "And moving fast."

"Let's hope Berat hasn't taken her phone and thrown it into a passing bus," Ellis said.

Riley's heart was racing. Never had he been so perturbed on a mission. "We will follow the tracking device. He's obviously got the copper scroll and he wants Abigail to translate it."

"I wonder if he's working for Vortex?" Ellis said as he swung to avoid a bird that nearly flew into the car.

"Could be, or he could be working for himself. Did you notice he said he knew Murat, but Murat said he didn't know the person who possessed the next clue? Eymen, Murat, and Berat were likely in some sort of group together. Berat wants to protect the treasure."

"But given that he's taken Abigail, it means they don't know the translation of the copper scroll yet," Thatcher pointed out. "Doesn't that strike you as strange? I mean, if the copper scroll's been in their possession for generations, wouldn't you think they'd have had it translated at some point?"

"You'd think so," Riley said. He scratched the stubble on his chin. "Maybe they didn't want to know where the treasure was—they just wanted to prevent others from finding it."

"That doesn't make sense," Thatcher said.

For once, Ellis agreed with Riley. "Berat is a fanatic. We've all dealt with fanatics before. Until now, he didn't want to know where the treasure was in case somebody tortured him to reveal the location. That's the typical attitude of this type of fanatic."

Thatcher nodded slowly. "You could be right."

"Can't this vehicle go any faster?" Riley asked urgently.

Nobody answered him. His stomach was churning. If this man was a fanatic, as they thought, then he wouldn't let Abigail live after she had translated the scroll. Riley went cold all over.

Just then, he lost the tracking signal.

"What now?" Ellis said. "Maybe we should go back and search Berat's place after all."

"All right then," Riley said, "but first we'll see if Murat is still there. I'll get the information out of him."

Ellis turned the car sharply and sped back to Selcuk. They parked not far from the knife shop this time, and Riley marched straight to the door. It was shut. That didn't surprise them given that Murat knew he was in danger.

"Let's go around the back," Riley said to the others. They had to walk past several stores before turning left into a small alley behind the shops. Riley had counted the shops, which was just as well as it was hard to tell which back entrance belonged to which shop. "That's Murat's knife shop there," he said. A broken padlock hung from the door.

Ellis pushed the door open. "Looks like our friends have already paid him a visit."

The three men slipped inside. Ellis wasted no time shutting the door behind them.

Once Riley was inside, he could see that someone had already searched the place. Papers were strewn all over the floor, and a desk was overturned.

"Well then, there's no point looking," Thatcher said. "Vortex would have already found anything by now."

"We're going to look anyway," Riley said. He knew his voice held a note of desperation, but he didn't care. With every second that passed, Berat was getting further away with Abigail.

Time was running out.

Riley pulled his phone from his pocket and studied it again. "Still no signal."

"Murat is long gone," Ellis said. He peered inside an empty safe. The door was open.

"All right, let's go back to where we were when we lost the signal, as we were heading in the right direction," Riley said.

"Shouldn't we search Berat's shop?" Ellis asked.

Riley's response was a curt, "No."

They drove back. All the while, Riley kept staring at his cell phone, hoping and praying the signal would come back on. It did not.

"This is where we were before. Do you want me to keep going?" Ellis asked him.

"Yes."

"What if the signal comes back and we have to backtrack?"

"We'll cross that bridge when we come to it," Riley said. He stared at the phone for a further five minutes, until suddenly the signal did come back on. "I've got it!" Riley exclaimed.

Ellis shot him a quick sideways glance. "We're out of gas."

Riley groaned aloud. "Could the timing be any worse?"

"We can go a few more miles, but we'll have to stop at the first gas station we see," Ellis said.

Riley leaned back in the seat. "Sure."

To his relief, there was a small gas station not far away. "I'll go inside and get some sodas," Thatcher said. "Do you want anything, Riley?"

Riley shook his head. All he could think about was Abigail. He kept staring at the phone. "Hurry, won't you?"

Thatcher returned to the car just before Ellis did. Thatcher handed Riley a soda and *simit*, a local circular bread.

"Still drive straight ahead?" Ellis said.

"Yes, I'll direct you," Riley said urgently. "The tracking came to a stop just after you got out of the car. We have a location now."

They soon turned off onto a smaller road, and after a mile or so turned off again onto a steep road that wound its way up a rocky hill.

"He's taken her to a remote location," Thatcher said.

The comment did nothing to soothe Riley's nerves.

A small wooden bridge marked the spot where

the road narrowed and became a rocky track. "We're getting close now," Riley said.

"What do you want me to do?" Ellis asked him. "Should we park here and go on foot?"

Riley leaned over to point to a clump of trees. "Go another half mile and then stop over there," he said.

Ellis hadn't gone quite half a mile when they saw a small hut up ahead, standing alone on the hillside. He immediately reversed the car and then pulled off the road behind a big boulder.

Riley was out of the car in a flash, his gun drawn, sprinting up the hill with Thatcher and Ellis hard on his heels. Riley was only halfway to the hut when he saw a man jump in the car and drive away in the other direction. Riley couldn't tell at that distance if the man was Berat.

He sprinted to the hut door and flung it open, his heart in his mouth.

14

EASTERN ANATOLIA
ONE HOUR EARLIER

ABIGAIL AWOKE IN A BLIND PANIC. SHE FOUGHT against a wave of nausea. It took her only seconds to realize she was in a trunk.

She hoped Riley was all right. Why had Berat gassed them all? And why had he abducted her? Was he a Vortex agent? But if so, why did he only take her?

Abigail was somewhat claustrophobic, but the trunk was large. She felt around inside for something she could use as a weapon but was unable to find anything apart from a large sheet.

A wave of terror overwhelmed her—was the man going to murder her and wrap her in the sheet before burying her? She fought to control her breathing as her throat constricted in fear. She tried to think logically. If he was going to kill her, surely he would have done so by now. He had abducted her. But why?

Abigail forced herself to think it through to take her mind off her fear. The man had seemed interested in the fact that she could translate ancient Greek. Was he taking her to the scroll? Or did he have the scroll all the time? Either way, the only thing that made sense would be if he had abducted her so she could translate the scroll.

Unless of course he was working for Vortex, although Abigail had no idea why Vortex would want to kidnap her. Surely they would already have translators in their employ.

She braced herself a little too late as the car went over a bump. She couldn't hear any noise apart from the roar of the car's engine. She had no idea if they were on a city road or a country road, but she couldn't hear any horns blasting or any trains or other loud sounds. At any rate, it would be logical for Berat to take her to an isolated location.

Abigail's mind went blank. It hurt simply to think. No doubt all her questions would be answered soon enough. She lay there, wishing the car would come to a stop and the man would tell her what was going on.

It was over an hour before the car did stop. Much to her alarm, the trunk stayed shut for several minutes. Was Berat taking care of some business there and then intended to drive on further?

Abigail didn't know whether to be afraid or relieved when the trunk finally opened. She blinked as the sun shone directly in her eyes.

"Now, I don't intend to hurt you, unless you do something silly," Berat said. "Do you understand?"

Abigail tried to nod, but a sudden sharp pain struck her neck and traveled all down her right side. She at once clutched her shoulder. "Yes," she said in a small voice.

"You can scream all you like and no one will hear you," he said, "only the bears."

"Bears?" Abigail repeated.

"Yes, there are bears in these hills," he said, "so don't even think about trying to run away. You won't get far, and I'm armed."

He pulled his jacket aside to reveal a gun.

Abigail trembled. "What do you want with me?" she asked.

The man looked surprised. "Isn't it obvious? I want you to translate the copper scroll."

"You have it?" Abigail exclaimed.

He didn't respond. "Wait there and don't move. I'll shoot you if you try to make a run for it." He walked over to the hut, looking back over his shoulder at Abigail as he went. Abigail hadn't noticed the hut until then. It was a rough stone building the same color as the rocks surrounding it.

He carried some crates out of the hut and placed them in the trunk. The word, 'Explosives' was written in English with Turkish words beside it.

Why was he loading explosives into his car?

Berat took her by the elbow and dragged her roughly over to the hut, and pushed her inside the door. He indicated she should sit on a couch that looked as uncomfortable as the one he had in his shop, only smaller.

Abigail sat on the couch, moving her neck this way and that, trying to relieve the pain from her cramped neck.

The man handed her a plastic bottle of water.

"Like I said, I'm not going to harm you. I just want you to translate the scroll."

Abigail rubbed her forehead with her left hand. "I don't understand. Who are you working for?"

The man frowned deeply. "Working for? I'm not working for anybody. For generation after generation, my ancestors have kept the Croesus treasure safe from marauders. Now this group, or organization, or whatever they are, has killed Eymen. This is the closest anyone's ever gotten to the copper scroll."

"But the men I was with are trying to keep those men from finding the copper scroll," Abigail said.

The man continued to frown. "I can see you believe that, but I don't share your confidence. What government agency wouldn't want that gold?"

"When I translate the scroll, and you find the location to the treasure, what will you do with it?" Abigail asked him.

"The word passed down from our ancestors to us is that the treasure is in a subterranean cavern. I need to find it so I can blow up the entrance, so no one can enter ever again."

"But they will simply excavate," Abigail said.

"I will make sure no one knows it's there."

A small trickle of fear ran up Abigail's spine. Was he saying he wasn't going to leave any witnesses? Did that mean he was going to do away with her too? Once she translated the scroll, she would know where the treasure was.

"What do you need to translate it?" he said. "Do you need some sort of dictionaries or something like that?"

"Quite possibly," Abigail said. "Still, I might be able to translate most of it."

The man lowered his backpack to the ground. He opened it carefully and produced a box. He opened the box to reveal another small box, and inside that was a small box carefully wrapped. The process reminded Abigail of Russian nesting dolls.

Finally, he put on a pair of cotton gloves and opened the last box.

He beckoned Abigail over. "The copper scroll."

Abigail gasped. Before her was an ancient artifact over two and a half thousand years old. It was magnificent.

"Don't touch it," Berat warned her.

"Of course not," Abigail said. She bent over it. "It's in good condition."

"We've been very careful with it," Berat said.

"What does it say?"

"It's inventory," Abigail said. It actually *was* inventory. She had planned to say it was, even if it wasn't. She had no intention of telling him the treasure's location. Anything but that.

"An inventory of treasure?"

She nodded. "It says the treasure is in five different locations, but the main location is inside the Temple of Artemis."

That was the truth, and Abigail considered it too vague for Berat to find the treasure.

"Go on," he prompted her.

"It's a partial list of treasure. Do you want me to read the items?"

"Not specifically," he said, "but give me an idea. You don't have to read the whole thing. Just get to the bit where it mentions the location."

"It mentions vast amounts of gold and treasure."

Berat clenched and unclenched his fists. "Quit stalling. Get to the location. It must be at the end."

Abigail pointed to where the scroll was broken. "It doesn't give the location at the bottom," she said. "It's still listing the inventory there."

The man's face flushed beet red. "You're lying!"

"I'm not," Abigail protested. "I'm telling you

the truth. You can see for yourself it's broken and if, as you say, the location is at the end of the scroll, then you can see for yourself that the scroll is broken before it reaches the end."

Berat put his face close to Abigail's. "You're lying," he hissed again. "I was told the scroll lists the location at the end."

Abigail looked at the scroll once more. "But it doesn't. There are two words at the end which might be a clue."

The man appeared to have lost his temper entirely. "What are they?" he yelled, completely enraged. He reached for Abigail's arm and twisted it behind her back, just as a shrill sound rent the air.

He dropped Abigail like a hot potato. He put the copper scroll back in the backpack, nowhere near as carefully as he had removed it, and ran outside. Abigail hurried to the door and watched him drive away.

Abigail had no idea what to do. It was then she realized her phone was still in her jeans pocket. She could have cried with relief. She pulled it out to call Riley when she saw a white SUV travelling up the dirt track at speed.

Was this Riley? Or was it Vortex? She had no idea.

Abigail was looking for somewhere to hide when the door burst open.

It was Riley. Abigail ran over and flung her arms around his neck. He held her close, stroking her hair. "Are you hurt?"

Abigail shook her head but didn't let him go. "No, he wanted me to translate the copper scroll," she said into his chest.

From the corner of her eye, she saw Ellis and Thatcher walk into the hut.

"Where's Berat?" Riley asked, still stroking her hair.

"He had an alarm. He knew you were coming. An alarm went off."

"He must've had an alarm on the posts at the bridge," Thatcher said. "Was he alone?"

Abigail nodded. Riley finally set her aside. "Are you sure you're all right?"

"Yes. He seems a bit of a fanatic, but he isn't working for Vortex. He said his family has been guarding the treasure for generations, even though he had no idea where it was, apart from the fact it's in an underground cavern. He has explosives with him. He's going to find it and blow up the entrance to make sure no one ever finds it. He also said he would get rid of any witnesses."

Riley looked angry.

Ellis and Thatcher had disappeared, presumably to search the vicinity.

"I actually saw the copper scroll," Abigail said.

"You did?" Thatcher said as he walked back into the room. "Did you translate it?"

Abigail nodded. "It said Croesus divided the treasure into five separate locations, but the main one was at the Temple of Artemis."

"At Ephesus?" Thatcher said, looking confused.

Abigail shook her head. "No. Berat said the treasure is inside the Temple of Artemis in an underground cavern."

"Maybe there's an underground cavern under the Temple of Artemis at Ephesus," Thatcher suggested.

"Yes, possibly," Abigail said. "There was a Temple of Artemis at Sardis as well, and Sardis was the capital of Lydia."

"So let me get this right," Riley said. "The copper scroll didn't tell you the location of the temple?"

"The scroll was broken at the end and it ended on two words," Abigail said. "They must be the clue to its whereabouts."

15

SELCUK

"No Amazons."

"DO YOU HAVE ANY IDEA WHAT THAT MEANS?" Ellis asked her.

After Abigail remained silent for a few moments, Riley said, "It might help to think out loud."

Abigail nodded. "Good idea. Two words—not much to go on. The Temple of Artemis at Ephesus had a large frieze depicting the Amazons—you know, the famous mythical warrior women. And there's a strong connection with Croesus as well. He made very generous offerings to the Oracle at Delphi as well as generous donations to the rebuilding of the temple of Artemis at Ephesus. Herodotus wrote that Croesus paid for many of the columns, so it's not known whether he paid for the entire temple to be rebuilt as well. Archeologists did discover a column drum with the inscription 'Dedicated by Croesus' on it. What's more, there are Lydian inscriptions from the time of Croesus mentioning the cult of Artemis."

"What remains of the Temple of Artemis at Ephesus today?" Thatcher asked.

"Not much at all, I'm sorry to say," Abigail said. "Basically, just a huge column. There's not much at all to see."

"Do you think that's what the reference to the Amazons meant?" Thatcher asked her. "The fact that the temple was destroyed?"

"But it wasn't destroyed at the time of the copper scroll," Abigail pointed out. "It would have been still standing." She tapped her chin. "I think I know what it is!"

She looked up to see three impatient faces. She

pushed on. "Croesus was fond of helping the Greeks—he consulted the Delphic Oracle and he rebuilt the Temple of Artemis, either in whole or part."

"You've already said that," Ellis said with barely veiled impatience.

Abigail waved one hand at him in dismissal. "No, I'm getting to the point. The Amazons were depicted on the frieze at the temple at Ephesus because legend states they fled there when escaping from Hercules. There was also a Temple to Artemis in Sardis, Croesus's capital."

Ellis interrupted her once more. "Does it depict Amazons?"

"It's not standing today," Abigail said, "but I very much doubt it depicted Amazons. There was no geographical link to them as there was at Ephesus. Some ancient writers did suggest there was another Temple to Artemis, a subterranean one, in which Croesus hid most of his treasure."

"Sounds like looking for a needle in a haystack," Riley said.

Abigail shook her head and tried to quell her growing excitement. "No, that's just it! When I was a doctoral student, I knew a scholar who started to excavate at Sardis, but he ran out of funding and couldn't get any more. He went on to dig at Jezreel and then Dor because it was easy to get funding for those sites. He told me he had, in fact, uncovered evidence that there was a subterranean Temple to Artemis near Sardis. He published on it."

"What did he say?"

"He only mentioned some small finds, but he said it was located above the Pactolus River. When I was a doctoral student, I was his research assistant on the Lydian dictionary. I still have my email correspondences with him."

"Can you search them on your phone?" Riley asked.

Abigail clutched her stomach. "Yes."

"All right, let's go. Let's find a café somewhere where we can eat and decide what to do next."

Abigail could see that neither Ellis nor Thatcher approved of such action, but they didn't say anything. "Find one on a busy street," Riley said to Ellis.

Abigail pulled out her phone, but Riley shook his head. "Wait until we get there," he said softly.

Abigail had no idea why, but she nodded.

As soon as they walked inside the little café,

Riley said to Ellis, "Get a table. I want a quick word with Abigail."

Both Ellis and Thatcher hesitated but walked away.

Riley waited until they were out of earshot. "Abigail, when you look through your emails, don't say aloud what you find. I want you to show anything you find to me, but don't tell the others. Also, don't mention the professor's name in front of them."

"Why?" she asked.

Riley frowned, and at first Abigail thought he wouldn't answer. After continuing to frown for some time, he did. "I don't know who to trust."

Abigail was shocked. "You mean you don't trust Ellis or Thatcher?"

"I don't trust anybody," Riley said. "Something is just not right about this situation and it's making me uneasy. So when you find the emails, show them only to me."

"What if they ask me about them?" Abigail said.

Riley patted her shoulder, sending electric tingles running through her body. "Leave that to me."

His hand remained on her back as he guided her to the table.

Abigail logged into her email on her phone and then tried to set the search for years earlier. It wasn't as easy as she thought it would be. She was still searching when the food arrived.

"Aren't you going to eat?" Riley asked her.

"I have to find it first," she said. It took her a while to find the emails, given they were years earlier, but once she found the group of emails, it wasn't hard to find the one she was looking for. She swiped to make the text bigger, and read the entire email.

Professor Briggs said he had uncovered a site of tomb robbers killed by an earthquake. With them were gold figurines depicting Artemis as well as gold brooches containing seeds linked to the cult of Artemis, and this led him to believe they had robbed a nearby Temple of Artemis. He had also found a cave entrance, which he believed was a subterranean entrance to the Temple of Artemis.

Briggs said he had discovered the cave entrance on the day he was to leave, so he didn't pursue it any further, and of course, he didn't return when he couldn't get any funding. He'd asked Abigail to keep the information to herself because he didn't want robbers to go in there and remove artifacts illegally.

Abigail couldn't believe her luck. She tried to mask her features as she handed the phone to Riley.

"Found something?" Thatcher said.

Riley answered for her. "Possibly. I'll tell you when we're back in the car." He put Abigail's phone inside his jacket pocket.

Abigail was too excited to eat, but she didn't know where her next meal was coming from, so forced down mouthful after mouthful. The men ate a hearty meal while watching the road. Abigail noted that the car was within sight of the window at all times. Maybe Riley was afraid someone would put a tracking device on it.

As soon as they finished their meal, Riley paid and they hurried outside to the car.

"Where are we going?" Ellis said when he jumped behind the wheel.

"You'll see soon enough," Riley said. "For now, head to the Izmir Airport."

Ellis turned back to the front, but not before Abigail saw a scowl on his face. Thatcher too looked angry; she could tell from the set of his jaw.

Riley pulled out Abigail's phone and took screenshots of her emails. She watched as he emailed the screenshots to his own phone. He then put her phone back in his pocket.

Abigail looked at the two men in the front of the car. Riley wasn't sure if he could trust them. Her stomach churned. What if they were Vortex agents?

EN ROUTE: IZMIR TO OXFORD

To Abigail's dismay, the flight to Heathrow was going to be a long one. What's more, there was no direct flight; flights offered two stopovers or one. Riley selected the next flight out with a single stopover in Munich of two and a half hours. Abigail hoped the stopover wouldn't extend much more than that. She'd had her fill of long airport stopovers in her years as an academic, traveling to conferences to present papers on everything from Akkadian loanwords in Biblical Hebrew to the language of the *Book of Ben Sira*, Ben Sira being the Second Temple Period author of *Sirach*.

"Stay close to me at all times," Riley whispered in her ear.

She stood on her toes to whisper back. "Are you worried about Berat?"

"Yes, and others as well."

Abigail was worried about being in danger. She told herself to take it one step at a time: arrive safely in Munich, arrive safely in Heathrow, arrive safely in Oxford, and visit Professor Briggs. If she broke everything into steps, it didn't seem so daunting. And surely she would be safe at the airports and on the flights.

The flight from Izmir to Munich was uneventful, apart from the fact that one of the flight attendants appeared overly flirtatious toward Riley. Despite the fact he seemed oblivious and all but ignored the woman, Abigail's hackles rose. For all the woman knew, the two of them could be married, or at least dating.

Abigail must have drifted off to sleep at some point, because she awoke to find her head resting on Riley's shoulder, much to her embarrassment. "I'm so sorry."

"Any time! I don't mind at all."

Her cheeks burning, Abigail turned away so Riley wouldn't see her blushing. The plane was beginning its final descent so Abigail distracted herself with the fact she was close to the first step of arriving safely in Munich.

The airport at Munich proved to be magnificent. As they walked through Terminal Two, Abigail saw plenty of restaurants, bakeries, and snack options.

Riley strode along looking as though he knew where he was going. The others fell in beside him. He stopped at a restaurant decorated in an unusual way with narrow tree trunks throughout the restaurant. "It's usually crowded," Riley said, "so we're in luck. They have good burgers here."

The restaurant offered a direct view of the airport ramp and Abigail assumed that was the reason Riley had chosen it. She certainly hoped they hadn't been followed.

Abigail's stomach was a little queasy, so she ordered a vegetarian burger with red onions, sun ripened tomatoes, and fresh salad. The three men ordered grilled beef burgers with fries.

When the food arrived, Riley turned to Abigail. "Feel free to help yourself to my fries. They're sweet potato fries."

Abigail was about to refuse but decided to try one. "Oh, it's delicious," she said.

Riley pushed his plate across to her. "We'll share."

Abigail noticed Ellis rolled his eyes. Still, she didn't mind. She wondered what it would be like to be in a relationship with Riley, if he was a normal person and she was solely an academic and they were on a date. Warmth flowed through her body.

The cold light of reality followed soon after. They were there on a mission, a mission which could get them killed and already had nearly done so. Abigail at once lost her appetite and refused dessert, although Riley ordered waffles with vanilla ice cream and both Ellis and Thatcher ordered chocolate cake with chocolate ice cream and cream.

Abigail wished she could eat so much without putting on weight, but figured their excessively active lifestyle burned off the calories in no time.

After they ate, Riley cast a look around him and checked his watch. Given the hour, the place was all but deserted.

"Are you going to give us the name of this professor now?" Ellis asked him.

"It's too much of a risk, to be honest," Riley said.

Thatcher raised his eyebrows. "Have you even contacted him yet?"

Riley shook his head. "Not risking it. We'll make contact after we arrive at Heathrow."

"So he lives in England?" Ellis asked.

Riley simply gave a curt nod by way of response.

After the men finished eating, they ordered coffee. Abigail glanced at her watch and was pleased to see more time had passed than she had estimated.

Would Professor Briggs even be in the country? She wanted to google him to find out but hadn't had an opportunity to do so. She certainly couldn't google him with Ellis and Thatcher around. Nevertheless, she was certain Riley had it all under control.

And when they found Professor Briggs, would they take him back to Turkey so he could show them the entrance to the temple? She supposed so, but she was highly reluctant to put him in danger. Vortex had already killed her friend, Jason Hobbs, as well as Eymen Bulut. How many more would die?

And were the Vortex agents already on their trail? Was Thatcher surreptitiously reporting to them? Or was Ellis? Maybe both? Or perhaps Riley was suspicious of everyone. Maybe that came with the territory.

When they boarded the plane for Heathrow, Abigail continued to study other passengers. What did Vortex agents look like? She assumed they were fit people like the men she was now with. Consequently, she stared at every athletic person she saw. There were plenty of them on the flight, a fact which did nothing to ease her nerves.

Abigail was also certain by now that Vortex agents were following them so she could lead them to the treasure. She hoped they didn't already know about Professor Briggs and would make their way to him first and murder him. But how could they know?

Still, she couldn't help but worry.

The flight to Heathrow was bumpy, which made sleep difficult if not impossible. Abigail abandoned all hope of sleep and instead watched a movie. It was such a bad movie, she thought it must have been an old one until she remembered she had read a review for it only recently.

When they landed at Heathrow, Riley put a protective hand on her back as they headed for customs. Abigail's heart was in her mouth, but once more they passed through quickly.

"Where to now?" Ellis said.

"We're catching a train," Riley said. Minutes later, they were in Heathrow Central station, paying for tickets to Oxford.

"The professor lives in Oxford." Ellis said it as a statement, but raised one eyebrow at Abigail, no doubt expecting a response.

Abigail, however, did not respond. Instead she said, "How long will it take us to get to Oxford?"

"Just under two hours," Riley said.

"Are we going to book accommodation and freshen up first or speak to Abigail's friend first?" Thatcher asked him.

"I'll decide on the way," Riley said.

Once more, a pang of anxiety struck Abigail. It had been bad enough being in the situation before, but now she knew Riley didn't trust his agents. That certainly left an uneasy feeling in the pit of her stomach.

After half an hour on the train, Abigail stood up. "I have to use the bathroom."

"There's one just there." Riley nodded to his right. "We passed it in the way. Come straight back, won't you?"

Abigail nodded and walked to the bathroom. As she reached for the handle, she saw a sign, 'Locked for service.' Abigail pursed her lips and looked around. She wondered where the next one was, but as she was standing there looking at the sign, an elderly lady bumped into her.

"Sorry, love."

"Would you happen to know where there's another bathroom? A working one?" Abigail asked her.

The woman pointed in the direction opposite to where Abigail had been sitting with Riley. "At the end of the carriage."

Abigail wondered if she should go back and tell Riley, but considered she was being overly paranoid. She thanked the lady and proceeded down the carriageway.

It certainly was a distance and she had no idea the train was so long. Abigail was walking back from the bathroom through the third carriage when she had the sensation she was being watched. She spun around and saw someone duck out of sight.

What was she to do? There were not many people on the train and what protection would they be against an armed Vortex agent anyway? Abigail fought to control the panic threatening to overwhelm her.

The person was between her and Riley. At that time of night, the train was all but deserted. Should she sit on the seat next to the only people in that carriage, an elderly couple, and hope the Vortex agent wouldn't come looking for her?

Her heart was beating out of her chest. Abigail inched forward. A tall man with blond hair walked toward her. He was staring at her, but when she looked him in the eye, he looked away. Abigail looked around. Should she run away from him and maybe lock herself in the bathroom?

No, she didn't want to be trapped. She sat in a vacant seat and trembled. When the man approached, he hesitated ever so slightly, looked at her and then continued on his way. Abigail jumped up and walked quickly down the corridor.

Her breath was coming in short bursts. She picked up speed and then at once collided with a man.

"I'm sorry," the man said, although his tone was ice cold.

Abigail looked into his face and was certain she was looking into the eyes of a cold-blooded killer. She knew it wasn't logical to feel that way, but somehow she just knew. The man leered at her. She backed away from him and then strode down the corridor in the direction of Riley, watching out more carefully this time.

When she reached her carriage, Riley was already standing up. "I was just about to go looking for you," he said.

Abigail at once sat on the seat. Riley turned to her. "You're trembling."

She relayed everything that had happened in hushed tones.

Riley stood. "Stay here."

He took two strides to sit between Thatcher and Ellis. He spoke to them quietly at and it was obvious to Abigail he was telling them everything that happened. When he returned to his seat, he said, "They're going to look."

The train suddenly lurched and the lights went out. Abigail clutched Reilly's arm in fear.

Thatcher was already standing. "I'll go and see what's going on."

"It could be an attempt to get Abigail," Riley said. "I'll have to stay with her."

Ellis and Thatcher hurried away in opposite directions.

Abigail was concerned. She was certain it wasn't

simply a fault with the train, not with Vortex agents around. But what were they planning?

Abigail was already sitting close to a wall and Riley shuffled closer to her. She saw he was on full alert.

His phone rang and Riley answered it at once. He grunted a few times and then hung up. Turning to Abigail, he said, "That was Ellis. He said someone has fallen out of the train."

Abigail's hand flew to her throat. "Are they all right?" Even as she said the words, she knew the answer.

Riley shook his head. "I'm afraid not."

"You think it has anything to do with… you know who?" she asked in hushed tones.

Riley nodded. "I doubt it's a coincidence."

Abigail clutched his arm.

"Don't worry. I won't let anything happen to you. I promise."

Despite the predicament she was in, Abigail believed Riley. Still, she couldn't help but be afraid.

Ellis returned. "Any updates?" Riley asked him.

"No. Where's Thatcher?"

"He hasn't come back yet."

"I'll go and look for him," Ellis said over his shoulder as he walked in the other direction.

Abigail steeled herself in case a Vortex agent suddenly appeared on the scene. She sat, tense, for a full five minutes until Riley's phone rang again.

Riley simply grunted in the phone again before hanging up and turning to Abigail. "Thatcher is missing."

"What? Missing from the train?" Abigail could scarcely believe her ears.

Ellis came back at that point. "I've searched the whole train. He's definitely nowhere to be seen. Should we all get off the train and look for him? I don't know how long they'll hold the train here with the body."

"This could be a trap to make us get off the train," Riley said.

Ellis nodded. "I was thinking the same thing."

"You get off the train and look for him. Meet us in Oxford at the Turl Street Kitchen restaurant as soon as you can. Keep me updated by phone. And Ellis, watch your back."

Ellis disappeared.

"Thank goodness nobody knows the name of your professor," Riley whispered to Abigail.

"Do you think this is all because of him?"

Riley shrugged one shoulder. "I wouldn't be

surprised. Vortex might have taken Thatcher to get that information out of him, but he doesn't know."

Abigail's scarcely dared ask. She didn't want to know the answer. "Will they believe he doesn't know?"

Riley shook his head.

Things were going from bad to worse.

17

OXFORD

THE TURL STREET KITCHEN WAS A RESTAURANT right by the Bodleian Library. It was in a gorgeous Georgian building, although the farmhouse-style tables and bare floorboards afforded a more bucolic, cozy tone to the restaurant.

Abigail desperately wanted to visit the Bodleian Library. Memories of her time spent there poring over leather-bound volumes in the Duke Humfrey's Reading Room filled her heart with warmth, but Jason's murder now shaded her golden memories of the Bodleian.

Abigail, not for the first time, wished she could have visited under different circumstances. She was certainly on a wild ride. Only a few days ago, she had no idea she would be on another mission so soon. She had been entirely consumed with her paper for the upcoming conference. The organization of the conference had been out of her hands due to the concerted and somewhat underhanded efforts of Harvey Hamilton. That had turned out to be a blessing, given that she was now on the other side of the world.

Abigail was concerned for her neighbor, Mary Yoder. Mary would worry about her unannounced absence, although she'd had the foresight to warn Mary she might disappear without warning from time to time. "For work," she had said. Mary had looked puzzled at the time but was far too polite to push the matter. An Amish lady, Mary ran a Bed and Breakfast with her husband, Eli, and rented Abigail the cottage behind the main building. Thankfully, Abigail's cottage had electricity and Internet as the bishop had long ago granted the Yoders permission to connect both due to the nature of their business.

She sighed, envious of the Amish for a moment,

their simple ways, their peaceful yet hardworking way of life.

Abigail pulled her coat around her and forced herself to study the menu. "The haddock fish fingers, chips, and pea puree and tartar sauce look good."

"I don't like fish." Riley turned up his nose. "I don't think I'll try this haddock stuff."

Abigail scooped the menu out of Riley's hand. "What about the beetroot, courgette—I think that's a zucchini?—and goats cheese tart with mixed leaf salad?"

Thankfully, they had arrived at Turl Street Kitchen without further incident. Ellis had called to say he had found Thatcher and they were on their way. He didn't give any details.

Before they ordered, Ellis and Thatcher turned up. Thatcher looked the worse for wear.

"What happened?" Riley asked him.

Thatcher sat down heavily and put one hand to his head. "I don't know, to be honest. I don't remember a thing. They hit me over the head pretty hard, I guess."

Ellis looked exhausted. "I found him wandering around near the train. They must have pushed him out of the train."

Thatcher's smile was rueful. "Luckily for me the train was standing still when they did."

"And lucky we avoided police attention," Thacker added. He stopped speaking when a waiter approached their tables.

Riley ordered the soup of the day with freshly baked bread and butter for his entree, and Abigail ordered the same.

Ellis appeared displeased. "That's a thing, you know."

Both Abigail and Riley looked up. "What is?" they said in unison.

Ellis narrowed his eyes. "Mirroring. It makes the person you are mirroring feel accepted and it forms a bond with them. Maybe, Abigail, you figured if you mimicked Riley's order, then he'd like you a little more."

Abigail's jaw dropped open. Riley merely grunted. His stealing a hunk of her bread saved her from thinking up a response.

Thatcher shot her a sympathetic look.

For the main course, Abigail selected the haddock, while Riley had the breast of chicken, new potatoes, green beans, olive salad with herb dressing. Abigail strategically chose the fish knowing Riley didn't like it, so she wouldn't have to suffer any more of Ellis's snide remarks. She thought about ordering a glass of chilled Pinot Noir, but she couldn't bare sitting across from Ellis as he scowled at her choice of beverage. She ordered a ginger beer.

After the main, Riley lowered his dinner fork. "I'm getting the dark chocolate brownie, white chocolate sauce and crème fraiche for dessert"

"Same," Abigail said without thinking. She inadvertently glanced at Ellis who shot her a smug smile but thankfully remained silent this time.

"In fact," Riley continued, "I think we should also both get the lemon posset, mixed berry compote with shortbread and the selection of cheeses with crackers and chutney."

Abigail was delighted Riley enjoyed desserts. She disliked men who didn't order dessert at a restaurant. She'd dated one such man, a long time ago. Their relationship didn't last long.

On the drive to Professor Briggs's cottage, Abigail wished it wasn't dark. She wished she could see the afternoon sun kiss the thatched roofs of the small white houses as they passed by. England was nothing if not picturesque.

Professor Briggs lived on the outskirts of a small village south of Oxfordshire.

"Err, just a bit of a warning—the professor likes cats," Abigail said as they drew nearer to the cottage.

"How many cats does he have?" Thatcher inquired.

"Just one as far as I know," Abigail replied. "And he's eccentric. You know those old jokes about absent-minded professors? Well, that's him."

Abigail knocked on the door. There was a note on the door, something about not letting the cat out written in beautiful cursive, but Abigail was too nervous to read it. After all, she had been the professor's research assistant back when she was a student years ago, and the reverence she had for him had never left her.

The professor opened the door. "Abigail! Is that you?"

"Yes…"

He interrupted her. "But why didn't you call? You're a long way from home. Still, I'm delighted to see you. Come in."

Abigail was dismayed to see that Professor Briggs was in a wheelchair. A cat jumped from his lap and scooted past Abigail.

"William Shakespaw isn't allowed outside," Briggs called out.

Riley scooped up the cat and returned him to the professor's lap.

"Thank you, err…"

"Riley."

"He's a lot cuter than your usual type," the professor said.

Abigail was aghast. "He's not my boyfriend, Professor."

"Thanks," Riley muttered. "Also ouch! You didn't have to say that so quickly."

Thatcher chuckled, while Ellis simply grunted.

Abigail found herself blushing furiously as the professor showed them into his sitting room. She soon forgot her own embarrassment when she saw the room was in a terrible state of disarray. She wondered who was looking after the professor, if anyone. She could not ask him in front of the men and embarrass him, but she made a mental note to do something about it.

Riley introduced the men. The professor smiled and nodded at everyone. "I'll make us a cup of tea and you can tell me why you're all here."

The professor accelerated his electric wheelchair to the kitchen to make them all a cup of tea. He presently returned with a tray balanced awkwardly on his lap. Abigail found it hard to take the tea, because William Shakespaw had taken a liking to chewing on her fingers. Riley had to hold her teacup while Thacker tempted the cat off her with a treat.

"I must admit," the professor said, stirring his tea, "when I saw you on my doorstep I was a little shocked."

"It's about your dig at Sardis," Abigail said, looking at Riley.

He took the hint and showed Briggs his I.D. "I'm afraid a terrorist group, or rather, an organization that funds terrorist groups, is close to discovering the location of Croesus's treasure."

The professor gasped. Riley pushed on. "There's a copper scroll that states the treasure was kept in five locations. The bulk of it was kept in a Temple of Artemis."

Abigail was keen to explain further. "I saw the copper scroll and it's broken, but there were two words before the break: 'No Amazons.'"

Briggs nodded. "So, not the Temple of Artemis at Ephesus."

Abigail nodded. "That's exactly what I thought. And we've been told it's a subterranean temple, so we wanted to know the location of the tunnel you found."

The professor stroked his beard. "I was certain that a tunnel led to a subterranean Temple of Artemis. Is this why poor Jason died? Such a nice young lad."

Abigail had a lump in her throat. "Yes, sadly."

"He was coming to see me, you know."

The three men were at once on full alert. It was Thacker who spoke first. "What did he say?"

The professor set down his teacup. "He wanted to ask me about my time on the dig near Sardis. He sent me a package."

"What was in it?" Riley asked urgently.

The professor shrugged. "No idea. I haven't had a chance to collect it yet, not with my leg. He sent it to my Post Office box."

Riley shifted in his seat. "Professor, please don't mention the location of the Post Office box aloud, not yet, in case there are surveillance devices. And Professor, I need you to come with us to Sardis. I need you to show us where the entrance is."

The professor looked down at his wheelchair. "My days of exploring ancient ruins are long over, boy. Besides, you wouldn't want an old man slowing you down."

"It's just we don't know the location of the entrance, Professor," Abigail said gently.

"I can give you directions. Better yet, I can draw you a map. You there—Ellis—can you reach that atlas?" He gestured to a wall of bookshelves. From where Abigail was sitting, she could see works by Aristotle, Plato, Homer, all the Greek playwrights, as well as Herodotus's *Histories*. 'Histories' was actually an ancient Greek word, which meant 'Inquiries' in English. English had taken the word 'histories' straight from the Greek. Herodotus was practically a contemporary of Croesus, having been born sixty or so years after Croesus's demise.

The professor gestured wildly. "No, the other one. Yes. This book has been in my family for a hundred years," Briggs said, taking the atlas from Ellis. "I'll write it all down in here."

Abigail looked at the page with dismay. "That's a bit too general. We'll need something more specific than that."

Briggs jabbed his finger on the open page. "There's a dusty track south of the archeological site. Keep going along it until you reach the Temple of Artemis. Of course, there are ruins of a Byzantine chapel inside that temple. Were you aware of that, Abigail?"

Before Abigail had a chance to respond, Riley

stood up. "Ellis and Thatcher, would you go outside and make sure we weren't followed?"

They left, looking none too pleased. Riley turned to Briggs. "Professor, we're running out of time. Could you tell me precisely where the tunnel is?"

"I'll do better than that." Briggs pulled some photographs from the pages of the atlas. "I took several photos so I'd be able to find it again." He handed them to Riley.

Abigail looked over his shoulder.

Briggs nodded. "I've marked the correct entrance with a red pen. All those other tunnels you see are simply tunnels to the Acropolis North. I was just starting to excavate those tunnels when I found disarticulated human bones along with plenty of gold jewelry. The evidence suggested they were robbers who had fallen victim to an earthquake. It made me think here was a repository of treasure directly under the Acropolis."

He muttered to himself. "But no one agreed with me. They were too busy looking for burial mounds under Karnıyarık Tepe in the Great Cemetery."

Riley rolled the photographs carefully and tucked them in an inside pocket of his jacket.

"Professor, may I have the key to your Post Office box? We will return the key and the contents of the box to you as soon as possible."

Briggs pointed to a wooden key holder hanging next to the front door. "The key is in that. Bring it to me, would you?"

Riley did as he asked. The professor extracted the key and handed it to Briggs. "Do you have any idea what Professor Hobbs sent you?"

Briggs shook his head. "He didn't say. He sent a text saying it was something I'd find of interest."

Ellis and Thatcher walked in the front door. Thatcher caught Riley's eye and shook his head.

"Professor, thank you," Riley said. "I'm afraid we will need to extract you for your own safety. It shouldn't be for too long, though."

"Oh dear." The professor hugged the cat close to his chest. "What about William?"

Riley looked thoughtful for a minute. "Yes, the cat can go with you."

"Everything will be fine," Abigail assured the professor. "I trust Riley with my life."

"If you trust Riley with your life then why aren't you dating him? You clearly think he's a dashing young man."

Thatcher boomed with laugher. Ellis rolled his

eyes. Riley cleared his throat awkwardly, but when Abigail finally had the courage to look at him, he did look pleased with himself.

"Will my cat and I be going to a pleasant place?" the professor continued. "Maybe a place with roses? I do love roses."

Riley stood. "You had best gather your things, Professor. You'll be leaving soon."

"I understand," the Professor said as he left the sitting room, wheeled out by Ellis.

Riley made a call. He didn't say much, but Abigail overhead him request they put a vase of roses in the house for the professor.

18

OXFORDSHIRE

"IT'S A GOOD THING THAT OLD PROFESSOR LIVES in such a remote location," the leader said to his men. "Remember, we need to take him alive and unharmed. We need him for backup in case the woman doesn't lead us to the treasure."

The agents were huddled in the heavily wooded landscape of the Chilterns.

"What about the agents sent to extract him?" Number Five asked him. "Do we need to take them alive too?"

The leader ground his teeth. "You ask stupid

questions. Obviously, you don't need to keep them alive. Why would you need to keep them alive? They don't know anything of any use to us."

"They know the location of at least one of RHTF's safe houses," the man said.

"So?" The leader jutted out his chin in a belligerent manner. "Does Vortex care where their safe houses are? No. Do *we* care where their safe houses are? No. We're here to follow orders and that's all. We're here to get this professor and take him unharmed. Understood?"

"Yes." Number Five appeared suitably chastened.

The leader shook his head. Vortex had informed him that the RHTF agents were on their way to Professor Briggs's house. In fact they were no doubt speaking with him now. The leader idly wondered how Vortex had accessed the information. Maybe the professor had a Facebook page. Everybody did these days, it seemed. It certainly made all the intelligence agencies' work a lot easier.

Now, with a broken leg and confined to a wheelchair, Professor Briggs wouldn't be showing anybody any international locations. That meant he would be extracted and taken to a safe location.

RHTF had already extracted Eymen Bulut's widow, much to the leader's irritation. And he hadn't been able to get his hands on Murat either. That man had disappeared off the face of the earth, but given his trade in petty illegal weapons, the leader wasn't surprised.

He wondered what sort of vehicle they would use to extract the professor. He hoped the other agents with the woman would go in a different direction, because he certainly didn't want to deal with them. And he needed that woman out of harm's way for the moment, so she could lead them to the Croesus treasure.

The leader's eyes lit up as he thought of the vast repositories of treasure. He trembled with excitement. The treasure had to be worth billions of dollars. Vortex were paying him handsomely for this and promised him a bonus if he delivered the treasure.

And, the leader thought, he would give himself a nice bonus. Vortex would never know if some pieces of gold jewelry were missing from the treasure, given no one knew how much treasure was there in the first place.

Now all he had to do was make sure he got his hands on this professor. Apparently, the professor was old and feeble and unable to defend himself. That made the leader's job easier. He figured there would be two people accompanying him and his men would outnumber them.

He looked around. "Don't slacken off, any of you! Are you ready?"

The men all answered in the affirmative.

"Now remember, the professor can't be harmed. He's elderly and frail so whatever you do, don't intimidate him. We don't want to give him a heart attack. If he dies, we'll have to answer to Vortex." The leader gave an involuntary shudder.

"But won't just the sight of us give him a heart attack?" Number Five asked.

The leader ground his teeth. Maybe in the mêlée he would shoot Number Five and report to Vortex that the RHTF agents had killed him. He smiled to himself and nodded, leaving Number Five's question unanswered.

He looked at the tree lying across the road. He afforded himself a smug smile of satisfaction. There were two roads leading from the professor's house. One road was a rarely used lane and that lane was where they now waited. He was betting the RHTF agents with the woman wouldn't go this way. He certainly hoped not. If they did, it would ruin his entire plan.

The leader shivered with the cold. He wasn't partial to English winters, but at least it was the end of winter and it wasn't snowing. Still, the bite to the air suggested it might sleet at any moment.

For all his skills, patience was not one of them. The leader hopped from foot to foot to stay warm while letting out a string of obscenities.

He was beginning to wonder whether the extraction teams had taken the professor on the other road, when he saw lights approaching. "Positions," he called. "And don't act until you make sure it's them. We don't want to shoot civilians and draw the attention of the local constabulary." He added those words for Number Five's benefit. The man really was an imbecile. Still, he wouldn't have to worry about him much longer, one way or another.

The large van screeched to a halt when it rounded the corner and came upon the tree trunk lying across the road. The driver immediately threw the car into reverse, but someone shot out the tires.

The leader was furious. Hadn't he just made a speech about identifying the occupants of the vehicle? He would lay odds Number Five was the culprit.

The four men ran to the car while the leader took cover by a beech tree. The windows were tinted and the leader was unable to see inside from his position.

The two front doors opened and he saw people roll out. The doors immediately shut and the lights flashed, signaling that the car had been locked remotely.

The leader swore under his breath. Gunfire was exchanged and he dived behind the cover of the beech tree.

The leader ran for the back of the vehicle. He knew the agents were out of the vehicle firing on his men and his men were firing back. Nobody knew he was there. He figured he could gain entrance to the front of the van through the back doors.

He crept up behind the vehicle. He inserted the crowbar between the bars, then, bracing his foot against the door, he heaved with all his might. Despite the cold, sweat broke out on his forehead from the exertion. The doors opened a crack. With one more wrench of the crowbar, the doors flew open. The leader smiled to himself as he climbed inside.

He was relieved to see the professor was unharmed. The elderly man was sitting, partly obscured by a green and blue tartan blanket, on a wheelchair secured to a bar behind him.

The professor lifted his head and reproduced a gun from under the blanket.

It took the leader a moment to realize that he'd been had. This was a decoy professor in a decoy vehicle. He'd been careless and had let his guard down. He had committed the cardinal sin—he had under-estimated his opposition. Now he was about to pay the price.

The gunfire stopped just as another vehicle arrived. The man pretending to be the professor jerked his gun at the leader, signaling him to move to the Chevrolet large-size van directly behind the van they were now in. The leader and his men were bundled unceremoniously into the back.

There was no sign of Number Five. Maybe he had run away.

The leader clenched his fists into balls.

19

OXFORDSHIRE

WHEN THE CALL CAME, RILEY WENT INTO THE kitchen to take it. He had stayed at the professor's house to wait for the news. Otherwise, they would be en route to the post office, and he didn't want Thatcher or Ellis to overhear the conversation with the extraction team. Apart from his professional duties, Abigail's safety was foremost on his mind.

"Thanks," he said into the phone before hanging up. His expression was grim. It was just as he had suspected, although the thought brought him no relief.

One problem presented itself: how was Vortex getting the information? Was it from Ellis or Thatcher—maybe both? How else would Vortex know their moves? Thankfully, he alone had known about the decoy extraction team.

The professor's house clearly hadn't been bugged because Vortex hadn't known about the professor, not until Riley's visit. Riley cast a glance around the kitchen. It didn't seem as though the professor had entertained visitors lately. Piles of unwashed plates were stacked on the countertop, emitting the unpleasant odor of stale food waste. There were no pizza boxes or other signs of takeout. Riley wondered what the professor had been eating, until he noticed the trashcan was overflowing with half-eaten frozen meals, the uppermost ones spotted with mold. Ants circled the bowl of half-eaten cat food on the floor.

At least the professor was safe, and it had been the decoy vehicle that had been ambushed. Riley was glad the agents were unharmed. The RHTF team had apprehended four Vortex agents, but one had gotten away.

He shook his head. At least Professor Briggs was protected and on his way to the safe house where he would have a decent meal, maybe for the first time in weeks.

When Riley marched back into the living room, three pairs of eyes looked at him expectantly. "The vehicle en route to the safe house was ambushed."

Abigail was at once horrified. "Is Professor Briggs all right?"

Riley hurried to reassure her. "He's fine. Our agents had decided to have a decoy vehicle and that was the one that was ambushed."

Abigail now looked thoroughly confused. "What do you mean?"

It was Ellis who answered for her. "I assume Briggs was taken in another direction to another vehicle. The Vortex agents chased the decoy vehicle thinking Professor Briggs was in it, whereas he was on his way to another location via another route."

Riley gave a nod of affirmation. "That's right. And he's perfectly safe."

Both Ellis and Thatcher frowned at Riley. There were barely perceptible frowns, but Riley recognized them for what they were. He was aware they knew he suspected either or both of them. If they were innocent, then the fact they were suspected wouldn't go over well, but if they were guilty, they would be angry that Riley suspected them. It was a no-win situation.

"What do we do now?" Abigail asked.

"We take the key and go to the post office," Riley said. "And I'm not going to say the name of the post office aloud just in case there is some kind of surveillance device on us."

Abigail yawned widely and stretched. Riley's heart went out to her. He was tired, so he couldn't imagine how tired a civilian must be. He didn't like to put her through this, but time was running out. He couldn't risk Vortex agents reaching the post office before he did.

And it seemed the Vortex agents had been ahead of them every step of the way.

Riley drove around in a circular route to the post office. He kept checking the maps app on his phone. He didn't want to use the GPS in the car because that would alert Thatcher and Ellis to their destination.

Finally, when Riley was satisfied he wasn't being followed, he drove to the little village post office.

It was dark and the street was deserted. Riley stepped out of the car and looked around. He couldn't see anyone, but what's more, he didn't feel anyone in the vicinity. Years as an agent had honed his intuitive skills. He opened the door for Abigail, held out his hand, and said, "Let's go." He could have opened the post office box, but he didn't want to leave Abigail alone with Thatcher and Ellis. He also didn't want to risk Abigail going anywhere alone.

Abigail opened the post office box without difficulty. Riley sighed with relief. So far, so good.

"Back to the car," he said, still looking around the street.

When they got back in the car, Riley left the engine running. "Open it now."

Abigail took some time to open the package, given that it was well wrapped. When she looked inside, she gasped.

"What is it?" Thatcher asked from the back seat.

"I don't think it's anything that can help us."

"Why don't you tell us and let us be the judge of that." Ellis still had the same snarky tone.

Abigail pulled out a book and handed it to Riley. "It's a book of Greek translations of sixth century Lydian ostraca. It was written over a hundred years ago, so the information isn't up to date."

"A wild goose chase then," Ellis grunted from the back seat.

Riley handed the book back to Abigail and drove away, after punching an address into the GPS.

"What now?" Ellis asked him.

"I know we have to get to Sardis in a hurry, but no one as yet knows the location. I doubt Vortex know as much as we do. We'll need some sleep. We'll stay in a hotel tonight."

His words received no argument. Abigail sighed with relief. She had been running on adrenaline, but now the very mention of sleep made her realize just how much she needed it. Her nerves were on edge and she was exhausted. She probably needed to sleep for a week but a night's sleep was all she was going to get. Still, she was grateful for that.

Abigail dozed off a few times and awoke when she hit her head on the side of the car. It was too dark now to see the scenery. She only realized she had slept when the car stopped.

Riley got out of the car. Abigail looked around at the Bed and Breakfast in the quaint little village. The others got out of the car, so she followed suit.

Riley took everyone's suitcases out of the trunk. "We should split up," he said to Ellis and Thatcher.

"You two stay here and Abigail and I will book into a B&B around the corner."

"Are you going to take the car?" Thatcher asked.

"You guys won't need it?"

They both shook their heads. Riley put Abigail's and his suitcases back in the trunk. "I'll meet you back here in the morning at seven," he said.

They drove around the corner and Riley parked the car. Abigail looked out the window at a big sign, 'White Stag Bed and Breakfast.' It looked nice enough, but she really didn't care. She would have been happy to sleep in the car at that point.

Riley took the luggage out of the trunk once more. "We're catching a taxi," he told her. "We're going to the next village. It's just a precaution."

Abigail thought that a little strange, but she didn't say anything. Sleep was uppermost on her mind. "How far to the next village?"

"It's probably about thirty minutes or so." He leaned closer to her and said in low tones, "I can't be certain there isn't a tracking device on that car."

They walked the short distance to a local pub and sat at a table while Riley called a taxi. "It'll be here in five minutes," he told her.

The rest was a blur. Abigail could barely keep

her eyes open. The very act of staying awake became a physical effort for her. She tried to focus on the traditional English pub interior: the low ceilings, the rough wooden beams, the whitewashed walls, but the lazy drone of conversation lulled her to sleep.

The taxi deposited them in at a Bed and Breakfast in a sleepy village. The sign outside announced there were vacancies.

Riley took Abigail by the arm, escorted her in, and asked the lady who met them in the lobby if they had a vacancy for two rooms.

The friendly woman was most accommodating. "Americans, are you? Well, I'll have to take your passports. Not that I think you're criminals or anything, but it's the law." She chuckled.

"That's perfectly all right," Riley said. "We'll be leaving before seven in the morning."

"That's fine. The first breakfast is served at six. Do you have any allergies or food preferences?"

"No. Riley looked at Abigail. She shook her head.

"Here's the breakfast menu. If you could just fill out the forms and drop them in this box here." She tapped a large wooden box with a slot in the top.

"We can have a nice cooked breakfast ready for you at six."

Riley paid and thanked the woman, who smiled before disappearing through a side door. Abigail was sitting on a chair by the reception desk, already dropping off to sleep.

"What would you like for breakfast?" Riley asked her.

Abigail opened one eye. "Anything at all."

Riley filled out the form for her and dropped it in the box. "Come on, I'll walk you to your room. I'll collect you at exactly six. Set the alarm."

"Um, err," was all Abigail could manage.

Riley showed Abigail to her room, and unlocked the door for her. "Again, don't answer the door to anyone except me at precisely 6 tomorrow morning."

"Sure." She walked into the room.

"And Abigail, lock the door behind me."

"Sure," she said again. She shut the door and latched the chain.

Abigail threw herself on the bed and immediately fell into a deep sleep.

She awoke sometime in the night with a start. She jumped out of bed and turned on the light. The door was still locked. All of a sudden, Abigail didn't feel tired at all. She hurried to the adjoining bathroom and looked at herself in the mirror. The shock itself was enough to jolt her awake. Her hair was sticking in all directions and was frizzy. It looked as though a goat had chewed on the ends. Deep semi circles of shadows sat under her eyes, both of which were somewhat bloodshot.

She took a long hot shower and looked in the mirror once more. There was an improvement, but now her face was beet red. Abigail shrugged. Her face was the least of her concerns. She climbed back into the bed and pulled the heavy blanket over herself. She did her best to fall asleep, but this time sleep eluded her. Now she was wide awake.

Abigail gave up. She sat up and reached for the book Jason had sent Professor Briggs. What was so significant about this book?

The scholarship was well out of date. Jason wasn't a lexicographer, but he didn't need to be, to know that. And it wasn't a nice rare volume either. Abigail couldn't figure out why Jason would send it to Professor Briggs. She flipped the pages and then held the book upside down and shook it in case there was a message inside. There was not.

Yet there had to be some significance. Abigail

stared at the book once more. She knew Jason—he wasn't in the habit of sending gifts to people.

She shook her head. No, this book had to hold a clue somehow.

Abigail was about to give up in disgust. She turned the book upside down one more time and shook it. Nothing fell out. "Just as I expected," Abigail said aloud, but then she noticed writing in red ink inside the book.

She read the writing and gasped.

20

OXFORDSHIRE

*The Temple of Artemis is under
the Acropolis North under
what I believe is the site of
Croesus's palace complex.*

ABIGAIL WAS ELATED. THAT INFORMATION, ALONG
with the photos, would pinpoint the location of the
tunnel. She knew that the sectors *ByzFort* and *Field
49* were believed to be the site of the Lydian
palace complex, and that the palace under the
Acropolis North was a different palace complex,

but this did not matter to her. The clue was that the Temple of Artemis was under the Acropolis North.

And now Abigail knew why nobody had discovered the tunnel entrance. She had been looking at drone footage of the site only the other week. Visible were several exposed sections of the tunnel that connected the Acropolis North with the dry stream-bed that once ran between ByzFort and Field 49.

Abigail couldn't wait to tell Riley, but it was just after 3 a.m. She was sure she would not be able to sleep, but lay back on the bed and shut her eyes, willing sleep to come. She awoke with a start when her alarm sounded, five minutes before six. Abigail climbed out of bed, more slowly this time, rubbing her eyes. She didn't feel refreshed at all—rather, she felt as though she needed another good night's sleep.

Riley knocked on her door at precisely six as she knew he would. She was ready. Abigail took in his clean-shaven jawline, his broad shoulders, his bright blue eyes. Butterflies coursed through her stomach.

"You look refreshed," Riley said.

That was the closest to a compliment he had ever given her.

"Thank you." Did she imagine it or did his face flush slightly?

"Breakfast?" he said rather too briskly as he turned on his heel and led the way down the corridor.

Abigail was more alert now and was taking in her surroundings. A Scottish coat of arms hung on the wall directly opposite the entrance to the dining room. The dining room was tiny, just enough room for two booths at right angles to each other. Currently, it was empty.

The lady must have noticed Abigail looking around. "The other guests won't have breakfast until eight. You have the room to yourselves."

Abigail shot her a smile before sitting down. She hadn't noticed the lady's Scottish accent until now. She had, however, noticed Riley sat with his back to the wall as he always did.

"Coffee?" The woman hovered over them, holding a stainless steel coffee pot.

"Yes, please!" Abigail said more forcefully than she intended. The aroma of freshly brewed coffee was delightful.

The woman laughed and filled both cups. When she left the room, Abigail looked around to make sure nobody could hear and leaned across the table. "I know exactly where the entrance to the tunnel is." Her voice ended on a note of triumph.

Riley looked shocked. "But how?"

Abigail looked around the room once more before sliding the book across the table to him. She opened the page with the writing and jabbed her finger on it. "Look what it says!"

"And you know where the Acropolis North is?"

"I do," Abigail said. "Can I have your iPad?"

He reached into his backpack and fetched the iPad for her.

She typed on it for a while and then slid it back to Riley. "This is drone footage of the Acropolis."

She watched his face as he registered what he was looking at. "What are all those tunnels?"

"Those are cross sections of the tunnel that ran between the Acropolis and a dry stream-bed. There are several tunnels under Sardis. In 1964, archeologists uncovered a network of Roman tunnels dug by ancient tomb robbers. They were only wide enough for one person." She tapped her finger on the iPad for emphasis. "These go under a burial mound to the chamber of what is presumed to be a member of the Lydian royal family. No chamber has been found as yet, despite archeologists digging over one hundred meters of tunnels."

Riley raised one eyebrow.

Abigail took that as a signal to continue. "And guess who wrote about these tombs and chambers centuries ago? Hipponax, the Ephesian poet who lived around the time of Croesus. Hipponax was Jason's area of expertise."

"Surely people have translated Hipponax before."

Abigail chuckled. "Hipponax's Greek was slang. It was a mixture of Greek, Lydian, Phrygian, and some Anatolian. Anyone trying to translate what he wrote as straight Ionian Greek would get it wrong, badly wrong."

Riley set down his fork. "So what does that mean in practical terms? I take it we don't go into those tunnels we saw on the video?"

Abigail shook her head. "No, not one of those tunnels, but we do go into a nearby tunnel. The writing in the book along with the photographs will show us exactly which tunnel it is."

Riley nodded slowly. "I see. We go to the cliff face where all those tunnels are and then the photos Professor Briggs gave us will guide us to the exact spot."

Riley looked the closest to excited she had ever seen him. He pushed on. "And that's why no one would have taken any notice of the tunnel if they had seen it before. They would simply think it was one of those tunnels that go between the Acropolis North to the—what did you say again?"

"Dry stream-bed," Abigail supplied. "Exactly! I discovered this around two or three in the morning and I was too excited to get back to sleep."

"Don't mention this to Ellis or Thatcher." Riley stopped speaking as the lady re-entered the room with two plates laden with food.

As soon as she left, Riley pushed on. "As I said before, let's keep this information to ourselves. The fewer people that know, the better. We won't tell anyone, including Ellis or Thatcher, until the very last moment."

Abigail's initial excitement was replaced with apprehension. She had almost forgotten she was in danger. "Riley, are you sure Professor Briggs is all right?"

"Yes, he's perfectly fine, no need to worry. He's in the safe house with his cat." Riley laughed. "Four Vortex agents were apprehended."

"How many of them were there to start with?" Abigail said.

"They're not certain as yet, but at least one did get away. "

"That's good, right?" Abigail looked into Riley's face hopefully. "Just one on the loose?"

"I'm afraid not. Vortex will send more agents."

Abigail's face fell. "So they have a never-ending supply?"

"Pretty much."

Her stomach sank. Riley was taking plenty of precautions, but was she in fact safe? How long before the new Vortex agents would arrive? Or did they know she was headed for Sardis and were there, waiting for her to show up? It wasn't the excavation season so they couldn't pose as archeologists. It wasn't the tourist season either, but there would no doubt be tourists at the site. Maybe the Vortex agents would be there after all, posing as tourists.

Despite the warmth of the food she was eating and the hot coffee, Abigail was unable to suppress a shiver.

They caught a cab back to their car parked outside the Bed and Breakfast and then drove it to meet Ellis and Thatcher. As soon as the car stopped, Ellis and Thatcher materialized and hopped in the back seat.

Riley drove off immediately. "They will anticipate we will drive straight to Heathrow, so we should take two cars and drive to Manchester airport. I'm driving to Carterton now to hire another car. It's west of Oxford, so Vortex won't expect us to go in that direction. Leave us in Carterton, and then the two of you proceed to Manchester, but stay off the main roads."

"Where and when will we meet you?" Ellis asked.

"I'll call you," Riley said. "For now, head for Manchester airport and wait there until you hear from me."

"That's a bit vague," Thatcher complained.

"That's all you're getting." Riley's tone was firm.

Abigail turned her attention to the quaint villages. The thatched roofs on the picture-perfect cottages fascinated her. When they reached Carterton, Ellis and Thatcher drove away. Abigail wasn't sorry to see them go. Ellis's disapproval of her was a constant source of irritation. Not that she was able to relax, given the circumstances, but it would certainly make things easier for her if his mood improved.

Abigail leaned back in the comfortable seat.

Driving in Britain, on what to her was the wrong side of the road, was disconcerting. She ducked several times when cars passed on the narrow road, much to Riley's amusement.

They were driving through another little town filled with quaint brick buildings covered with ivy, when a car rammed them.

21

OXFORDSHIRE

THE CAR WAS A RANGE ROVER, BLACK, WITH tinted windows. Abigail heard a scream—was it her own voice?—when it slammed into their car, ramming them off the road and into a tree. Glass from the impact peppered Abigail.

Someone dragged Abigail out of the car. It was a strange man. No, it was Riley. His face was covered in blood, but she could still see those eyes—those staggering, fierce eyes. He was barking orders at her, but she couldn't hear a thing. Her ears were ringing, and even though she might have been able to read his lips if these were calmer circumstances, she couldn't now. Not with her eyes all blurry from the impact.

Seemingly giving up communicating with her, Riley yanked Abigail to her feet and tossed her over his shoulder. He carried her out of the car and down an alleyway at speed, escaping for a moment the occupants in the Range Rover. How many had there been? Abigail couldn't say. She'd not seen a single one of them. She'd only seen Riley.

Riley finally set Abigail on her wobbly feet. She watched as he took a quick inventory of their surroundings. They were in the shadows of old buildings. In front of the buildings, intermittent traffic coursed along the road. On the other side, a quiet park saw families gathering for picnics and to walk their dogs.

There was no shelter in the park, and walking along the busy road would be crazy. They would be sitting ducks. Abigail could not believe they had been attacked in broad daylight, in a public place. Maybe they could go back the way they came, and call Thatcher and Ellis for help.

"Here."

Riley grabbed her elbow and heaved Abigail through a vaulted archway. They'd found themselves outside a museum. A man was busy arguing with a young woman.

"I'm sorry, but we're closed until next Tuesday," the man said in weary tones.

"But my daughters want to see inside," the mother complained. "You're here now. Can't you allow them inside for just a moment? As the curator, you have the power."

"I'm not here to open the museum. I was just here *momentarily* because I'd forgotten my book." He showed her a small paperback.

The twin girls were running past the man, into the museum. The man took off after them, as did their mother.

"Come on." Riley took Abigail's hand, and the two of them slipped upstairs, unseen.

At the top of the steps was a storage section cordoned off with red velvet rope, and it was in this section that Riley decided they should hide. Who would come looking for them there? No one.

Abigail fell back against the wall, grabbing her head and panting. Riley slipped off his jacket and rolled up his sleeves. "Are you all right?"

"Why wouldn't I be all right? It's not like a car rammed us." Abigail did her best to keep the tears at bay.

"We need a place to hide for a few hours," Riley whispered to her. "The Vortex agents will keep looking for us for a few hours. They won't give up easily."

"Why don't you call Ellis and Thatcher?"

Riley shook his head and winced. "No, it's best if we act independently of them for several hours. We'll rendezvous with them at the airport."

They heard the woman's voice at the front doors. She was yelling at her children.

Riley guided Abigail to the wall. "We can hide behind these huge storage jars with octopi on them."

"It's octopodes."

Riley's mouth fell open. "Sorry?"

Abigail hurried to explain. "Octopus is an ancient Greek word meaning 'eight feet'. The plural of 'foot' in Greek is *podes*. People wrongly apply Latin plural rules to the word, and come up with the dreadfully wrong word *octopi*." She shook her head sadly.

His lips twitched. "Always the academic! Maybe

you could explain it later. For now, we have to hide behind these jars with, um, sea creatures on them."

Abigail was embarrassed, despite the fact Riley appeared amused. They hid behind the jars, which had the added cover of a large display board sitting on the ground in front of them, seconds before they heard footsteps coming up the stairs.

"It's probably the curator," Riley whispered.

Abigail gulped. Yes. It was surely only the curator, but why had he returned?

Then a voice spoke, the tone disturbingly sing-song and menacing. "Come out, come out, wherever you are."

Abigail grabbed Riley's elbow. That voice didn't sound like it would belong to the curator. Abigail had gotten a good look as they passed him by—he was old, with white hair and a pink face. This voice sounded young and vital, if also chilling.

"I saw you come in here," the voice said again. It took a moment for Abigail to place the location of the voice.

Abigail momentarily froze. She caught a glimpse of a young man—younger than the curator, at least. His expression was troubling, a sinister smile and dead eyes. In a flash he raised his gun, but

Riley was even faster. He tackled him to the ground with a crash, sending the display board flying.

Abigail tried to stand, but pain shot through her ribs. She didn't think anything was broken, but the bruising was enough to push her back against the wall with a grunt of pain. Riley and the man wrestled on the ground as the man reached for his gun, which Riley had knocked across the floor to a plaster imprint of a dinosaur's foot. Abigail tried to grab it, but the man kicked out at her.

"Stay back!" Riley called to her. The man shrugged him off and grabbed his gun, raising it at Abigail. Riley threw himself in front of her.

A gunshot rang out.

For an awful moment Abigail stared at Riley's back, expecting him to crumple. But when the sound of a body impacting the polished floors echoed through the museum, Riley was still on his feet. Abigail looked beyond Riley's shoulder. The man had shot the curator.

It took Abigail several moments to process what had, in fact, happened. The figure was not the curator but a life-size mannequin of Winston Churchill. Riley was still on his feet and it was the Vortex agent who had been shot in the skirmish.

Riley checked the man's pulse and then looked over at Abigail. "He's dead."

Abigail didn't know whether to be relieved or upset. All she felt was panic.

"Stay here and hide. I'm going to check the rest of the museum."

Before he left, Riley dragged the man into another room and left him there. Abigail was happy he was out of her sight, but she felt sick seeing the dead man. She stood and moved to the other side of the room, just to get away from all that death.

Riley returned ten minutes later. "I found these frozen dinners in the kitchen. I microwaved them. We should eat where we can. We don't know how long we'll be holed up here."

Abigail didn't want to eat when she had just seen a man die. The thought of it turned her stomach. What's more, she was sick and sore. But when Riley opened one, revealing honey chicken, her stomach rumbled furiously. She accepted the meal from Riley and at once spooned some into her mouth. The food afforded her a measure of comfort.

"Will there be more of them?"

"Yes, but I have no idea when or if they'll find us," Riley said.

"That's not very comforting."

Abigail and Riley finished their dinner in silence. Riley pulled Abigail toward him and they both cuddled up together for warmth.

She awoke slowly. A telephone was ringing somewhere in the museum—a shrill, angry ring. Abigail pushed Riley's arm off her. She was dismayed to see a big, angry bruise on his forehead.

She tiptoed through the museum, checking to see if anyone else was there. After she made sure she was alone, she followed the ringing downstairs.

She meant to pull the phone cord out of the wall. She didn't want the ringing to wake Riley, who clearly needed the rest. As she did so, a voice called, "I see you, Abigail."

Abigail snapped her head to the side. The entrance to the museum was a big glass door, and on the other side of the door, stood a man about the same age as the dead man upstairs. He knocked a gun twice against the glass and grinned.

"Hello, Dr. Spencer. How is your boyfriend? Oh, don't tell me; he's dead?" The man's voice was just as chilling as his associate's. "The same fate does not have to await you."

"Why is that?" Abigail asked. She tried to keep

the tension and fear out of her voice, but it cracked all the same.

This made the man smile. "I can help you, you know. I don't like killing women."

"How noble of you."

"Come on, we don't want to kill you. We can use somebody with your translation skills. Open the door."

It wasn't just a glass door that stood between Abigail and the man. There were bars too. Abigail turned and ran upstairs.

Riley awoke as soon as she reached him. He grabbed Abigail by the shoulders and pulled her toward him. "Are you okay?" he asked urgently.

"They've found us. There's another man downstairs."

"Did he see you?"

"He spoke to me," Abigail said as she helped Riley stand.

"What? How?"

"The phone was ringing. It woke me up." Abigail felt stupid telling Riley this. She should have just let the phone ring out. "I pulled it out of the wall."

"Why?"

"I was afraid it would wake you. I thought you

might have a concussion. A man spoke to me. Then I looked over to the door and he was standing there. Riley, he has a gun."

"Yeah," Riley said. "So do we. Let's go."

"Where?"

"To the airport. Come on." Riley walked over to the window and pushed it open. It took a little bit of rattling, but it opened in the end. Riley helped Abigail onto the museum's rooftop.

They scrambled over to the edge of the rooftop and glanced down. The neighboring building wasn't too far down, and it was connected to the museum. Riley helped Abigail down and then he lowered himself after her.

With adrenaline once more pumping through her veins, it was impossible for Abigail to know how hurt she was. Her ribs pinched a little, but that didn't stop her from crossing the rooftop and clambering onto another.

On the third rooftop, Riley let Abigail take a quick break. She peeked over the edge and saw two Range Rovers in the street below. Her friend at the door had no doubt made the call to his associates. They knew they were in the area, so they needed to move fast. "I'm fine now."

"No, you're not."

"Look."

Riley glanced over the ledge and saw the Range Rovers. "Yep, you're fine," he said, hustling her once more along the rooftops. They managed to get down to the ground through an apartment building, slipping into a bedroom through the open window and then slipping out the front door.

Riley managed to hail a cab as soon as they hit the street.

The driver didn't ask any questions about their rumpled and bloodied appearances, because he in all likelihood didn't care, and because he was on the phone to his wife yelling about credit card charges. Closer to London, they stopped at a public bathroom to clean up.

"They'll think we're still at the museum," Riley said as they finally arrived at Manchester airport. He paid the driver and then hurried Abigail inside.

It took them about fifteen minutes to rendezvous with Thatcher and Ellis, who were eating donuts and drinking coffee.

"What happened?" Thatcher said. "I've got medical supplies. You look like you both need patching up."

"A car hit us pretty hard," Riley told then. "Did you have any trouble?"

"We were tailed by several Vortex agents for a while. Where did you two go?"

"To a museum," Abigail said.

"We thought we needed the culture," Riley added.

Ellis snorted. "Yeah, well, next time stick to kombucha. Let's go."

22

SARDIS: MODERN DAY SART

ABIGAIL DIDN'T REMEMBER MUCH, IF ANYTHING, about the plane ride to Izmir, or for that matter, the short journey from the Izmir airport to the ancient site of Sardis. Her ribs were sore and her head hurt. The one major plus was that the flight from Manchester to Izmir was direct, and only four hours. She had drifted in and out of sleep all the way to Izmir, and fell back to sleep in the hire car, waking only when she heard the word 'Sardis'.

She looked out the window at the sheer cliffs of the acropolis and gasped at their magnificence.

Riley tapped Ellis on the shoulder. "Head north from the village and turn east to the ancient site."

"I know you have to pay separately to enter the Temple of Artemis and the gymnasium," Abigail told Riley, shaking herself awake.

"We're not here for sightseeing," Ellis snapped.

Abigail sighed. "I wasn't suggesting we were. I thought we should avoid those areas." She wished she could stay and explore the ruins of Sardis, but she would have to come back another time. *If* she got out of here alive, she reminded herself.

"I'll drive from here," Riley said. "Abigail, guide me to the cliff face with the tunnels."

Ellis stopped the car and the two men swapped places. Abigail didn't like sitting next to Ellis, but at least it wouldn't be for long. She realized Riley was driving as close as he could get to the tunnel's entrance and intended to give Ellis and Thatcher as little warning as possible.

A pang of misgivings hit Abigail. If anyone was following them, they were leading them straight to the treasure. Still, all she could do was follow Riley's lead, and she trusted that he knew what he was doing.

Abigail looked longingly at the ancient site and the reconstructed bath-gymnasium complex dominating the landscape as she directed Riley to swing the car down a dirt road. In ancient times, the gymnasium stood over five acres. From here, she could see the ruins of the synagogue, built around two hundred years after the *Book of Revelation*. It was one of the largest ancient synagogues ever found, and was in the center of the city rather than where most synagogues were, namely, on the edge of a city. She was awe-struck.

Sardis possessed a long and significant history. It had been the capital of the great Lydian Empire before the Persians defeated Cyrus, and then it had become an important Persian city, standing at the end of the Royal Road. Darius the Great of Persia built the Royal Road which started at the Persian capital, Susa, and ended in Sardis.

The distance between Susa and Sardis was 1,677 miles, yet the royal mounted messengers regularly covered the distance in nine days.

Abigail knew that Herodotus's comment on these couriers of two and a half thousand years earlier,

> *"Neither snow nor rain nor heat*
> *nor gloom of night stays these*
> *couriers from the swift*

>*completion of their appointed*
>*rounds,"*

was inscribed on the James Farley Post Office in New York City and is acknowledged as the informal motto of the United States Postal Service.

Abigail nodded to herself. She always liked to point out modern connections to her students.

Sardis was then conquered in turn by the Greeks, by the Macedonian Alexander the Great, and then by the Romans, under whose rule the population grew to 120,000.

If only she had time to take photos for her Biblical history students. The Book of Revelation states that Sardis had few worthy inhabitants. As for the others, Revelation says they have the reputation of being alive but are dead. It utters them a dire warning. At the date Revelation was written, Sardis was still a wealthy city. It had been destroyed by an earthquake fifty years earlier but had been rebuilt by the Roman emperor Tiberius.

Ellis's words brought Abigail back to the present. "I don't like the look of that."

She followed his gaze to see a scattering of tourists already at the site, taking photos in the early morning light.

The bumpy dirt road ended at a clump of rocks. Riley got out and stared at the photos, holding them up and comparing them against the landscape before him.

Abigail looked up at the massive rock face looming above her. How on earth did the Persians take the acropolis? Had a Lydian traitor let the Persians in through an access tunnel? No one had ever discovered the reason, and most likely never would, she mused.

"What are we doing?" Ellis said. "You're going to have to tell us, Riley."

"We're leaving the car here and going on foot," Riley said. "We'll need the night vision goggles and the chem lights."

Soon the men were donning backpacks. Riley handed Abigail some night vision goggles. She turned them over in her hands, concerned that they were so bulky.

"You'll get used to them," he said.

The sun beat down on them, reflecting off the rocky landscape. Abigail was afraid of what lay ahead.

"Care to brief us now?" Ellis asked.

"Sure," Riley said. "There should be a tunnel

somewhere here and it possibly leads to a subterranean Temple of Artemis."

"To the treasure?" Ellis asked, rather too eagerly for Abigail's liking.

"It's likely," Riley said.

"It's possible an earthquake blocked the entrance," Abigail told them. "There was a massive earthquake at Sardis in 17 AD, so it *is* an earthquake region."

She wondered what they would do if they found the tunnel impassable, but she figured Riley would call for backup. Really, she had no idea. She still wondered why they hadn't had altercations with Vortex agents since arriving in Turkey. And worse still, she didn't want to go into an underground passage. It crossed her mind to ask if she could wait outside but figured that would be too cowardly. Besides, they would need her if the place was booby-trapped.

Abigail hadn't heard of any Greek temples being booby-trapped, but then thousands of inscriptions were discovered every year, many of them at Ephesus. These inscriptions often provided new information about ancient times. She couldn't take any chances.

Abigail turned to Riley. "There are possibly booby-traps."

He nodded. "I thought as much. Any in particular we should look out for?"

Abigail shrugged one shoulder. "I don't have a clue, to be honest. I simply brought it up as a possibility. If this is where Croesus stored the bulk of his treasure, then it would make sense it was guarded in some way by something other than people. His wealth was legendary and he wouldn't have left it unguarded."

"This is the location Professor Briggs indicated," Riley said. "We'll look for the entrance to the cave now. Abigail, stick close to me. Let's keep each other in sight at all times."

Abigail looked around. To her left, the valley fell away to the Pactolus River, where the mythological King Midas was said to have washed away his gold. In front of her stood a hill of significant height. Some of it was impassable, but the passable section was nevertheless steep and rocky. She could see tracks left by goats.

"I don't need to tell you that the entrance to the tunnel won't be obvious," Riley said.

Abigail hoped Jason and Professor Briggs had

been right about the location. She didn't fancy spending a few hours wandering around, looking for a tunnel entrance. Ellis and Thatcher shimmied up the rocks at some speed whereas Abigail went far more slowly. She was fit and jogged most mornings, but she couldn't match the agents for speed and strength.

Riley helped her gain footholds as they scrambled from one boulder to another. It was hard going and soon Abigail was fighting for breath. She didn't want to look down but every now and then risked a glance. She would certainly do herself a terrible injury if she fell, although the going wasn't too steep. She just had to watch where she put her feet.

Ellis and Thatcher both disappeared around the edge of a boulder, earning a grunt of disapproval from Riley.

Abigail jumped as a scream echoed around the hills.

23

SARDIS: UNDER THE *ACROPOLIS NORTH*

THATCHER CLIMBED TOWARD THEM OVER A boulder. "Ellis fell!"

"Stay there," Riley said to Abigail, seconds before he vanished over the boulder with Thatcher.

Abigail stood there shaking. Was Ellis all right? And if someone as capable as Ellis had fallen, would she? Had a Vortex agent shot him? Were Vortex agents out there now, watching them at this very minute? Or maybe Ellis was a Vortex agent and had gone to report what they were doing to Vortex.

She sat down on the dirt and clutched a large rock with both hands, shutting her eyes tightly.

She had no idea how long she sat there, but finally she heard Riley's voice, "Abigail."

She opened her eyes. "Ellis?"

"We can't find him. We can't see any sign of him."

Abigail was shocked. "How is that possible?"

Riley shrugged. "He must've fallen into a crevice."

Thatcher was standing behind Riley. "I wasn't watching him when he fell. He'd gotten ahead of me. I only heard him scream and when I looked around, he wasn't there."

"What do we do now?" Abigail said. "Do we climb down and look for him?"

Riley shook his head. "He's likely at the bottom of a crevice. There's nothing we can do and we didn't see him at the bottom of the hill. We'll just have to keep going."

"He wouldn't have survived the fall," Thatcher added, "so there is no urgency to find his body."

Abigail thought that was a callous thing to say, but she kept her opinions to herself.

Riley took Abigail's arm and said, "Hurry. For

all we know, Ellis was shot. We have to keep moving."

Abigail's stomach clenched. She had thought of that possibility. That would explain why he fell. Maybe the Vortex agents had taken his body.

She kept climbing, higher and higher, spurred on by the thought she might be shot, when Riley said, "There."

Behind a large boulder Abigail saw the entrance to a tunnel. Given that it could only be seen at that angle, it was well hidden.

"Go in first," Riley instructed Thatcher.

Thatcher dropped to his hands and knees to crawl inside the small opening between the boulders. He disappeared from view. Moments later, he stuck his head out. "It's quite big in here." He reached out to his backpack and pulled it inside.

Riley went next and then waved his hand out the door, signaling for Abigail to go in. She steeled herself to crawl through the narrow space but once inside, was relieved to see the cavern before her was large. To her left was a pile of rubble no doubt caused by a previous earthquake. She expected the cave to smell musty and moldy, but the air was fresh and clear, with no scent.

Riley already had his flashlight from his

backpack and was shining it over the walls. Abigail saw a little stream of running water to her left and wondered if the running water kept the cave air odorless.

"Professor Briggs was right," Riley said. "There is indeed a tunnel. How on earth would he have discovered this place?"

"Probably from ancient texts," Abigail said. "The ancient Athenian soldier, Xenophon, mentions an altar to Artemis in the time of Cyrus." She would have said more, but Thatcher interrupted her.

"But we know about the Temple of Artemis at Sardis. We passed it on the way here."

Abigail shook her head. "Not a temple, an altar. No one has ever found the altar. Maybe Professor Briggs was looking for it. At any rate, he found the bones near the tunnel entrance."

Thatcher shone his flashlight over some boulders. "There's another tunnel there."

Abigail and Riley hurried over to inspect it.

"It does look like this tunnel goes for a fair way as far as I can tell." Thatcher cracked a chem light and threw it into the tunnel. "Hmm, just as I thought," he muttered to himself.

Abigail had hoped she would be able to stand

upright in the tunnels but no, it was just as she had feared. She would need to crawl. The Harvard expeditions had discovered Roman tunnels of this size running under the burial mounds in Sardis. Still, she had hoped for bigger tunnels under the Acropolis North given that Lydians had built these tunnels.

Riley placed his hands on Abigail's shoulders. "Now, it's the same as when we were in Greece. Remember what I said? I'll go first and if the tunnel gets too narrow, you can always back out. Are you all right with that?"

"Yes," Abigail said in a small voice, although she was anything but all right. She liked closed-in spaces even less than she liked heights. Still, she had no choice but to follow Riley and Thatcher.

Riley pressed the car keys into her hands. "Put these in your pocket."

A fresh wave of terror hit Abigail. Did that mean Riley thought he might not get out of there alive? She trembled violently.

As she stuffed the keys deep in her pocket, she felt something strange in the lining. "What's this?" She pulled off her jacket and handed it to Riley.

Riley picked up a piece of jagged rock and ripped the jacket open, producing a tiny black box.

"It's a tracking device. It must have been in your jacket the whole time. Who had access to your jacket? That is, since we left your college?"

Abigail thought for a moment. "No one."

Thatcher hurried over to them. "Berat must have sewn it in when he abducted you." To Riley, he said, "Berat must have intended to let her go so she could lead him to the treasure. It was his plan all along." He took it from Riley and crushed it under his boot. The two men exchanged glances. "That means he's on his way," Thatcher added, "with explosives. We have to hurry. Abigail, put on the goggles."

She did as he said, and blinked several times in succession. Everything looked spooky almost, a funny shade of green, but at least she could see.

The rock was cold and dark. Thatcher was already making his way along the tunnel. Abigail crawled as fast as she could, trying to escape the waves of claustrophobia that struck her, scared Riley would go too fast and leave her behind. She was also afraid the rocks would suddenly give way and she would plunge to her death into a bottomless pit. She knew it was an illogical fear, but it was a fear, nonetheless. And what if there was an earthquake? She would be crushed or trapped there forever. Her brow broke out into a cold sweat.

Abigail tried some self-talk to calm herself. The tunnel wasn't getting any narrower. In fact, it seemed as though it was getting wider. Maybe the Temple of Artemis was directly ahead. Still, that was no small comfort because it was underground. At that moment, Abigail wanted to be on the surface more than anything else.

Suddenly, Riley's boots vanished. Before she had time to panic, his hand reached for her. She crawled into another cavern, a smaller one this time, but at least it was bigger than the tunnel. Abigail trembled violently.

Riley put his arm around her and held her close. "Are you all right?"

"Yes," she lied. She was glad he couldn't see her face because then he would see just how frightened she was. He squeezed her tightly and then released her.

Diagonally opposite them to the right was a bigger tunnel than the one they had just crawled from. This one looked man-made. Thatcher made for the tunnel, but Riley put out a restraining hand. "There's an inscription above it. What does it say, Abigail?"

She walked up and shone her flashlight over it. "It appears to be a bilingual inscription: Lydian with a translation into Greek. I can't translate the Lydian without a lexicon, but the Greek says,

*'Beware. All who enter here to
steal the gold are cursed.'"*

"A curse?" Thatcher said. "That explains why the locals were too afraid to proceed."

"Curses have never prevented grave robbers over history from looting," Abigail pointed out.

Riley agreed. "I don't think anyone has gone past the first tunnel that we just came through in centuries. If your professor didn't do it, then I doubt anybody else would. Obviously, no one made the connection with the subterranean Temple of Artemis and the treasure of Croesus."

"Well, let's go into that tunnel. What are we waiting for?" Thatcher asked, eagerness evident in his voice. "The treasure could be just ahead of us."

"Not so fast," Riley said. "It could be booby-trapped. Are you sure there's not a deeper meaning to that inscription?"

"Not as far as I know," Abigail said. "I think it's safe to proceed."

"You *think?*" Thatcher said. "Then maybe you should go first."

"*You're* going first," Riley said roughly. "On your way."

Thatcher muttered something Abigail couldn't hear and then disappeared into the tunnel.

The next thing Abigail heard was a shriek.

24

SARDIS: UNDER THE *ACROPOLIS NORTH*

RILEY PULLED ABIGAIL AWAY AS BATS FLEW PAST her face. She could have cried with relief. She wasn't overly fond of cave-dwelling bats, but they were far preferable to Vortex agents.

Abigail realized she was clinging to Riley and he made no attempt to let her go.

"It was only bats," Thatcher called back to them, somewhat unnecessarily.

Riley released Abigail. He ducked into the tunnel and Abigail followed him. She shone her flashlight over the rough-hewn walls to get a better look than the night vision goggles afforded her. "Surely this must lead somewhere significant, maybe the temple," she told Riley. Her words echoed strangely.

"I thought as much," he said.

The temperature dropped as she crawled onward. If only she was back in her comfortable bed, or even giving a lecture—anywhere that was safe. She took a deep breath and forced herself to crawl further. Her knees were beginning to hurt. How far had she come? A hundred feet? More? She was completely disoriented with nothing around her but artificial green gloom, and the only sounds being her own breathing and shuffling sounds made by Riley and Thatcher.

Abigail heard Thatcher gasp and then Riley reached back and helped her into what she at first thought was a cave.

She stood up. She heard chem lights crack and shut her eyes at the ensuing blinding white light.

Abigail removed her goggles. She was struck speechless at the sight before her.

Directly in front of her were two large golden hippocampuses flanking the steps to an imposing marble-clad Temple of Artemis towering above her. She looked up in awe at the ancient building. "I can't believe it. I can't believe it," she said over and over again.

Riley and Thatcher seemed equally shocked.

Abigail, of course, had never seen a temple in its original state. She had only see ruins. Her eyes roamed over the giant marble columns. "It's an Ionic design the same as the Temple of Artemis at Ephesus," she said.

"What do you mean?" Thatcher asked her.

"Well, I mean not a Doric or Corinthian order," she told him. "The Ionic columns were more graceful than the Doric, and incorporated friezes of continuous sculptural relief."

She shone her flashlight over the friezes way above her head.

"So the treasure would be inside?" Thatcher asked her. "And look at those golden animals!" His flashlight traveled over the golden hippocampuses.

Abigail hurried to a column. "Look at the oak leaves and acorns on this column and snail scorpions and salamanders!" She was beside herself with excitement. It was just like going back in time over two and a half thousand years. No one in modern times had seen such a sight.

"Abigail, there's an inscription on the column,"

Riley said urgently. "Do you think it's referring to booby-traps?"

Abigail bent to peer at the writing, which was in Greek not Lydian. "No, those will just be the donors of the columns," she said. "It was common practice to record the donors' names on the columns."

"Do you think there are booby-traps?" Thatcher asked her.

"It's always possible," Abigail said. "I mean, this is a Greek temple, but Croesus wasn't Greek. Sure, he funded the Temple of Artemis at Ephesus, and like I said earlier, Xenophon mentioned an altar of Artemis from that time period, so maybe Croesus did follow the cult of Artemis. We know for certain that he made offerings to the Greek god, Apollo, at Delphi. There are no known booby-traps in Greek temples, but given that inscriptions with new information are being discovered all the time, maybe one day they'll find inscriptions saying there *were* booby-traps in Greek temples."

"In that case, we will have to proceed carefully," Riley said. "Does this look like a standard Temple of Artemis to you, Abigail?"

"I've only seen them in ruins, of course," she

said. "But yes, it does fit with the descriptions of other Temples of Artemis."

"In what section of their temples did they keep the treasure?" Thatcher persisted.

Abigail shook her head. Thatcher was just like one of her students, more interested in treasure than in ancient cultures and their social history. To Abigail, history *was* treasure. "Your guess is as good as mine," she said. "Temples typically weren't used for storage of mega amounts of treasure, but any treasure was normally kept in the *opisthodomos*."

"What are the sections of the temple?" Riley asked her.

"Sacrifice was always performed outside. People entered the temple through the columns into the vestibule, and behind the vestibule is the *cella*. Behind that is the cult statue of Artemis. Behind that is the *opisthodomos* and behind, that the *posticum*."

"English please," Thatcher said.

Abigail shrugged. Her eyes were still smarting from the brilliant white light after being so long in the tunnel. "No one knows for sure due to ritual secrecy. Sometimes the *opisthodomos* was the treasury although sometimes the word referred to the inner shrine. The *posticum* was the portico at the back, although sometimes the *opisthodomos* and the *posticum* were one and the same. The *cella* often included an *adyton* to house the statue, although *adyta* often also held sacred items."

"You really don't have a clue where the treasure would be held, do you?" Thatcher said, a snarky tone creeping into his voice. "It sounds as though you're just as confused as I am."

Abigail frowned. Thatcher was certainly departing from his previous pleasant demeanour. Before she could respond, he added, "I suppose you won't know unless we proceed. If it *is* booby-trapped, what sort of booby-traps could there be?"

"Could be anything. Could you get that flashlight out of my eyes?" She wondered why he was still using it when the chem lights illuminated the area so strongly.

"Sorry," Thatcher said, although his tone suggested he was anything but sorry. "These golden winged creatures must be worth an absolute fortune, a king's ransom in fact!" His voice rose to a high pitch. "I wonder how we'll ever get them out of here? Maybe we'll have to enlarge the tunnels, or maybe the roof of this cavern is close to the surface and we can drill. Have there been any earthquakes in recent times?"

"There was the big one in 17 AD. The Roman historian, Tacitus, reported that people were swallowed by the earth opening up. It was a massive earthquake, with the ground levels being significantly displaced and fires everywhere. There was no warning and it came at night. It affected twelve cities over eastern Turkey, but Sardis was the worst affected. This temple this has obviously survived it," Abigail added.

She was not at all happy with the thought of anyone removing the golden hippocampuses or doing anything to the temple. This was an archeological delight, an incredibly rare, preserved precious piece of ancient architecture. In that regard, it was priceless, even if it hadn't contained any gold.

"All right, let's proceed. Be careful, and Abigail, you stick close to me," Riley said. "Let's shine our flashlights over every dark place in case there are inscriptions warning of booby-traps. We can't be too careful."

Abigail agreed. "The Lydians built this, and we know very little about them. Maybe they did have booby-traps. Other cultures had things like streams of mercury, poisonous gas, steps that would give way to chasms, as well as the deadly mercury sulfide powder," Abigail cautioned them. "I wonder if we could throw rocks ahead of us to see if they trigger something. Of course, we would have to be careful that we don't damage anything."

Both Riley and Thatcher agreed, and soon the three of them picked up various stones and small rocks lying around the ground and threw them up the temple steps.

After an interval, Thatcher said, "Nothing's happened," just as Riley threw another rock.

At that moment, arrows flew out of the walls, about three feet into the air.

Thatcher froze on the spot. "Did you see that?"

Abigail clutched Riley's arm. "Booby-trapped crossbows are said to be hidden in the tomb of China's first emperor, Qin Shi Huang. Have you heard of him? He's famous for building the Great Wall of China and for the army of terracotta warriors."

Both Riley and Thatcher nodded, so she continued. "Today, most people think the crossbows are a myth, but the renowned Chinese historian, Sima Qian, who was born about sixty years after Qin Shi Huang's death, recorded that Huang's tomb was protected by lakes of mercury and booby-trapped crossbows. In recent years, archeologists discovered high levels of mercury in the soil surrounding the tomb, so maybe Sima Qian was right about the crossbows too."

Riley nodded. "In that case, we'll have to crawl up the stairs and keep low to the ground."

"It happened when your rock landed on that step there," Abigail said. "Riley, can you throw rocks on the steps either side of it?"

He did as she suggested, but no more arrows shot out. Finally, he threw a rock on the same step and arrows shot out almost too fast for Abigail to see.

Riley pointed to the step. "It might be just that step, but it's too wide for us to jump across, so we'll have to crawl up anyway."

Abigail was shaking. She dug her fingers into Riley's arm a little tighter and said, "That means there will be other booby-traps. That won't be the only type."

"Yes, I know that." Riley's tone was calm.

Abigail wondered how he could be so brave. She wanted to turn tail and run back to the safety of the outside air, to feel the sun's warmth on her face, and to breathe crisp fresh air rather than the eerie air of the giant cavern.

"What are we waiting for?" Thatcher said. "Come on!"

"Keep low," Riley said again.

It seemed to take an age. Abigail crawled along, keeping as low to the wide steps as she could. The marble felt cold under her hands and her knees were raw. She was in awe of the ancient building and at the same time, terrified for her life. She fought the panic as it came at her in waves and threatened to overwhelm her time and time again.

When they reached the top of the stairs, Abigail sat down and tried to steady her ragged breathing.

"Do you think there are more arrows or will there be a different type of booby-trap up ahead?" Thatcher asked her.

"I really don't know, but I'm sure there will be more."

"What type of booby-traps did they have in ancient tombs?"

Abigail scratched her head. "Oh gosh. Well, the crossbows were supposed to be a myth, but I guess we found out that they weren't."

"What about proven ones?" Thatcher pressed her.

"Many of them were used in warfare, like the explosive Chinese land mines from the thirteenth century." Thatcher's mouth dropped open as Abigail continued. "They used a rip cord or a pin that released falling weights. Those rotated a flint wheel, which created sparks to ignite the fuses for the land mines."

"See if you can find any inscriptions," Riley said to Thatcher.

"If you're looking for warnings, I don't think there will be any," Abigail told him. "Croesus and his men would have had no reason to warn anyone of the booby-traps."

"I'm sure you're right, but it won't hurt to check," Riley said.

Nevertheless, they didn't find any inscriptions warning of booby-traps, just as Abigail had predicted.

Riley and Thatcher cracked some more chem lights and threw them inside the building. Abigail wished there was electric lighting so she could take in the true magnificence of the structure. The chem lights were bright, but they were not pervasive.

When they carefully walked inside the building, Abigail expected to be impaled by an arrow at any minute. Her imagination was running away with her.

"What now?" Thatcher said. He stopped right by a fluted column.

"We proceed—carefully," Riley said. "Abigail, stay behind me."

Abigail didn't need telling twice. She certainly didn't want to go ahead.

She heard the sound before she saw anything. Riley and Thatcher heard it at the same time.

"Quick, retreat," Riley said. They ran back the way they had come. Abigail was going to keep running, but Riley caught her arm. She swung around.

To Abigail's horror, where they had just been standing was now a stream of silver liquid.

"What is it?" Thatcher asked.

"Mercury," Abigail said. "We must have stepped on something that released it. Archeologists have found mercury in at least four sites around Central America. They found a large quantity of liquid mercury in a chamber below the Pyramid of the Feathered Serpent in Teotihuacan, in central Mexico. And I've already told you about mercury in Qin Shi Huang's tomb."

"Enough of the history," Thatcher said. "What else are we likely to encounter?"

"Don't touch anything covered with red

powder, because that could be the deadly mercury sulfide I mentioned before. Apart from that, the only other booby-traps I know of are oil and liquid tar, and the ground suddenly opening up into a pit." She thought for a moment and then added, "And sometimes spikes come up from the ground."

Thatcher rolled his eyes. "Great! Well, so we proceed and look for the treasure? The mercury seems to have drained away."

Riley hesitated a moment and then said, "I would prefer to leave, but it's our mission."

They edged on ever so carefully until they came to the giant statue of Artemis.

"Wow," was all Abigail managed to say.

Thatcher seemed impressed. "Is the statue gold all the way through?"

Abigail shook her head. "I doubt it. One ancient writer said the cult statue at Ephesus was made of cedar wood, but others said ebony or grapewood covered in silver or gold. I'm surprised those crossbows still worked after thousands of years," she said as an afterthought. "Surely the cords would have been destroyed by bacteria by now or the metal mechanisms rusted."

"Maybe that's why they only worked on that

one step," Riley speculated. "Maybe the crossbows were supposed to work on every step."

Abigail shuddered. "I didn't think of that. Still, archeologists recently found chromate on weapons excavated with the terracotta warriors, and chromate would prevent the mechanisms from rusting."

"Let's keep moving," Thatcher said. "You said the treasure would be behind the statue?"

"In a normal temple it would be."

Thatcher edged forward, followed by Riley and Abigail.

There was a wide door in the wall behind the statue. When they reached the door, Riley cracked a chem light and threw it in.

The three of them gasped in unison.

25

SARDIS: UNDER THE *ACROPOLIS NORTH*

A BIGAIL COULDN'T BELIEVE HER EYES. Innumerable mounds of gold and treasure stood before her. There were solid silver stags as well as golden stags, piles of jewelry, and huge wooden chests that Abigail figured were full of gold items as well.

Thatcher was the first to find his voice. "It's here! I can't believe it!"

"Don't move," Abigail said. "This is surely booby-trapped."

Despite the light from the chem lights, the three

of them shone their flashlights over the walls and then over the ground. "What's that?" Thatcher asked, pointing to a stream of liquid silver in front of them.

"It's mercury again," Abigail said. "Whatever you do, don't touch it. I'm surprised it's here. Two Cretan architects, father and son, were responsible for the rebuilding of the Temple of Artemis at Ephesus in Croesus's time. Surely they didn't build this one, not with the booby-traps. I haven't heard of that type of technology from the Minoan civilization."

"Idle speculation is of no help in a time like this," Thatcher said.

"That's enough, Thatcher," Riley snapped at him.

Abigail thought that Thatcher certainly had seemed to develop a different personality. He had always been pleasant before, but now he appeared tense and moody. Maybe it was the stress of the booby-traps and the realization he could meet his death at any moment.

"We can cross over there," Riley said, indicating a small structure to his right. "There's a little bridge."

Abigail could smell the pungent odor of

mercury sulfide. She just wanted to get out. But for now, she had to try to stay calm. "No, see that red powder on the hand rails? That's cinnabar, mercury sulfide. If anyone touches that, they'll die. Maybe not right away, but they will die within weeks. It was used in the tomb of the Mayan Red Queen. I wonder who devised these traps for Croesus?"

"Like I said, now is not the time for academic reflection," Thatcher snapped. "Let's find a way across. We could walk across the bridge easily enough without touching the rails."

Before Abigail could suggest caution, he hurried across the bridge. She and Riley followed him.

"Now what?" Thatcher asked. "There's a drain in front of me."

"The drains would have been used to carry moisture away from the temple," Abigail said. "It's quite a common device in underground tombs, and this is an underground structure. Or maybe there's an underground stream and they directed it into the drains."

Riley shone his flashlight into the drains. "I'm guessing it's an underground stream. That would explain why the air in here is so fresh and well oxygenated, although maybe there's another entrance as well. Abigail, do you think this is simply necessary engineering and nothing to worry about?"

Abigail bit her lip. "I can't say for sure that it's not connected to a booby-trap somehow. But yes, it is a necessary part of an underground tomb."

Thatcher jumped across the drain onto a ledge. He cracked another chem light and threw it in front of the treasure, despite the fact the chamber was already well lit. "This would have to be worth millions, billions, even," he said. He ran over to a pile of gold jewelry and picked it up, before letting it run through his fingers.

He seized a handful of coins. "How much do you think these would be worth?"

Abigail stopped to stare. "One coin would be worth thousands, I'm sure, depending on its condition."

"One coin would be worth thousands?" Thatcher parroted. "There are hundreds, maybe thousands, of coins here!"

Riley helped Abigail across the drain, holding her wrist firmly. "Be careful of that large pit there," he said. "Keep well away from it."

Abigail shone her flashlight into the empty pit where the ground ended. "It's part of the drainage system, I'm sure."

"So we made it then!" Thatcher said. "We safely arrived at the treasure. That's the last of the booby-traps. Or maybe there were more and the mechanisms didn't work."

"Quite possibly," Abigail began, still shining her flashlight into the void. She would have said more, but she heard Riley's sharp intake of breath and looked up.

Thatcher was holding his gun on them. "Well, it's the end of the road for you two."

26

SARDIS: UNDER THE *ACROPOLIS NORTH*

ABIGAIL GASPED AND EDGED CLOSER TO RILEY.

"So you're the mole!" Riley said in disbelief. "What did you do to Ellis? Why couldn't we find him?"

"I hit him over the head and dragged his body to a spot between the rocks," Thatcher said. "I then screamed, pretending I was him, and told you he'd fallen over the edge. That's why you couldn't find him." He made a clicking sound of derision with his tongue.

"So, to clarify, you're working for Vortex?" Riley

said. "Or have you gone independent since you saw the size of the treasure?"

Thatcher sneered at him. "Maybe a bit of both! They won't notice any missing." With his free hand, he stuffed his pockets with gold coins as he spoke.

Abigail's hands were shaking from sheer terror. They shook so much her flashlight traveled over the marble floor at Thatcher's feet and caught sparkles in a thin vein of quartz. It was then she noticed strange striations on the marble floor to his left. At first, Abigail thought the green color was a result of silica impurities, but then she took another look.

Was that what she thought it was?

She squeezed Riley's arm and then stepped to her right a little, hoping he would take her meaning.

It seemed to work and he followed her as she edged away toward the pit.

"How long have you been working for Vortex?" Riley asked him.

Abigail was relieved that Riley was keeping Thatcher talking. If only he would be able to keep him talking long enough for her plan to work.

They edged further away until they were at an angle to Thatcher.

"What's it to you?" Thatcher said rudely.

"You don't need to kill us," Abigail said. "Will

you let us go if I give you the car keys?" She threw the keys onto the middle of the platform.

Thatcher was momentarily distracted. "Of course I won't, you foolish woman," he said. He stepped onto the platform and reached for the keys.

As he did so, the slab collapsed under him.

Abigail clutched Riley as Thatcher's screams echoed below them. "I didn't want him to die," she said in a small voice.

"I'm afraid it's too late for that—it sounds as though he's fallen a long way down," Riley said. "Come on, let's get out of here. Abigail, you did the right thing. Another minute and he would have shot us both. Are you all right?"

"Of course I'm not all right," Abigail said, dismayed that her voice was shaky.

"What you did was very clever," Riley said in soothing tones. "You saved both our lives. Now let's just get out of here in one piece."

They turned back and were about to walk over the little bridge over the mercury when they stopped.

Moving lights.

Voices.

Riley seized Abigail's arm and drew her to him. "Did you call for help?" she whispered.

"No. Quick, we have to hide."

Vortex had found them.

Abigail hoped there were no more booby-traps, but there was no more time for caution. Riley took her hand and pulled her over to the treasure. They both hid behind a large wooden chest.

Soon the voices were in the room.

"That's mercury," a deep voice said. "Don't touch anything. Where's Thatcher? Are you in here, Thatcher?"

The voices echoed around the cavern. "Thatcher," the man called again.

"Maybe he hasn't made it this far yet?" another voice said.

"Then who put the chem lights in here?"

"He texted that he found the entrance and disposed of one of the agents. He should have disposed of the others by now, but I don't know where he is."

"Maybe they all succumbed to one of the booby-traps," the other voice said.

"Possibly."

Abigail thought the owner of the deep voice did not seem at all concerned about Thatcher's possible demise. "Let's make sure no one is around. Shoot on sight."

Abigail tensed. There were too many chem lights in the chamber. There was nowhere to hide, nowhere dark. Not anymore. She looked over at Riley. He was holding his gun, but how many Vortex agents could he shoot at once?

And how many voices had she heard? Three? Four? And were there others who hadn't spoken? She had no idea. For all she knew, there could be an army out there. And how did they get past the booby-traps? Perhaps some of the men had fallen foul of the arrows and the mercury stream.

As soon as Riley took a shot, their position would be given away and the Vortex agents would come. He couldn't shoot them all at once.

Abigail sat there, terrified by her own thoughts. Riley signaled to her to stay down. Of course, she was going to stay down. There was no other option.

If only those chem lights weren't so bright.

Abigail realized she was holding her breath and let it out slowly. She kept very still. Riley crawled away from her a little and she looked at him in shock. Was she meant to follow him or stay where she was? Her mind wouldn't work properly. Thankfully, Riley indicated she should stay there. She nodded.

She watched as Riley crawled away and then

out of sight. Where had he gone? And would she ever see him again? What if he was shot and killed? She trembled violently. Her blood ran cold as a bout of dizziness overwhelmed her.

Abigail crouched lower to the ground, trying to make herself as small as possible.

She heard a sound and looked up, expecting it to be Riley. To her horror, a man appeared in front of her. A look of shock passed over his face when he saw her. She had no time to react before Riley hit him hard over the head. The man landed with a thud beside her.

Abigail spun around and stared at him. Riley held his finger to his lips and moved away again.

It was all too surreal. Abigail wouldn't have been surprised to have woken up and found it all had been a terrible nightmare.

Abigail sat there by the unconscious man, wondering what she should do if he regained consciousness and wishing she could tie him up. She realized Riley had taken the man's gun, but she was no match for a man of his size.

Abigail could hear footsteps, but no one was speaking. Maybe the Vortex agent had realized Riley was there and didn't want to give away their position.

A fresh wave of terror hit Abigail. Riley was hopelessly outnumbered. How would either of them get out of this alive? All she could do was sit there and watch the unconscious man.

She was flooded with relief when Riley crawled back to her. "I've taken out four of them," he said. "There are likely more out there. Could there be a back way out of this temple?"

"I have no idea. If it was simply a temple, then yes, but it's in a cavern. I have no idea if there is a back way out of this cavern."

"You're doing well," Riley said. "It's almost over now. All we have to do is find another way out and then everything will be all right."

Abigail shot him an incredulous look. He made it sound so easy, but she knew that the reality was far worse than he had indicated.

She pointed to the huge pile of treasure by the back wall. "There should be a doorway behind that wall," she said. "If there *is* a back way out, it will be through that door."

"We won't be able to use chem lights because if anyone's out there, they'll see us. Just use the night vision goggles, but we won't put them on until we're back in the dark. Okay?"

Abigail gave him the thumbs up.

Riley told her to wait and then crawled around the wooden chest. He nodded to her and indicated she should follow him. They both crawled quickly until they were behind the pile of treasure. It was only when Abigail stood up, she realized how sore her legs were. They cramped painfully. She stopped for a moment and dug her heels into the ground to try to relieve the cramps.

Riley held out his hand and she took it. They hurried out the doorway into the *posticum*.

There, standing in front of them, was a man with a gun.

SARDIS: UNDER THE *ACROPOLIS NORTH*

IT HAPPENED SO FAST ABIGAIL SCARCELY HAD TIME to take it in. Riley kicked the gun out of the man's hand. The man aimed a punch at Riley and within nanoseconds they were engaged in a fight.

Abigail stood back helplessly, not knowing what to do. She looked around anxiously in case the sounds attracted any other Vortex agents, but there were none. She noticed a statue of Artemis holding an iron spear. She tried to remove the spear from the statue's hand so she could use it as a weapon, but it was stuck fast. She picked up a beautiful jug, intending to hit the agent over the head if she could get a clear shot at him. Yet, try as she might, there was no opportunity.

The fight seemed to last forever. Abigail couldn't tell whether Riley had the upper hand. Both men seemed to be landing punches.

Riley stepped backward and then forward again. Abigail saw a slight movement under his foot, the white chem lights affording visibility. She took another look and saw the same striations on the marble that she had seen when Thatcher had fallen into the pit.

"The marble!" she called out to Riley. "Where you just had your foot. Just like what happened with Thatcher."

Riley gave no sign that he heard her, but he at once maneuvered the man onto the marble. The man grabbed Riley's neck, and for a horrible moment Abigail thought Riley would fall with the man into the crevice.

Riley lifted up both hands and moved them out and downward, thus breaking the man's grasp at the very moment the panel opened.

The man disappeared from view.

Abigail hurried over to Riley. His breathing was coming in ragged bursts. "You're bleeding," she said, touching her fingertips to the gash across his forehead.

"Good work," he said by way of response. "You did well."

Abigail opened her mouth to say more when a loud crack rent the air. She froze. "What was that?"

"Berat's dynamite! We can't go back the way we came. Let's look for another way out."

The exit was blocked. Abigail's stomach muscles clenched so hard they hurt. She went cold all over. Then a disturbing thought occurred to her. "That means any Vortex agents will head this way, looking for another way out too."

Riley nodded. "We have to hurry."

Abigail pointed to the striations on the marble. "See those marks there? Don't step on anything that looks like that."

"You can be certain I won't," Riley said.

He took her hand again, which made Abigail's heart flutter. She silently scolded herself for thinking about her attraction to Riley in circumstances such as these.

The two of them carefully made their way around the back of the temple. The illumination from the chem lights did not reach that far. Riley signaled that Abigail should put on her night goggles, and she did so.

They reached a corbeled arch, an entrance to another tunnel, without encountering any more booby-traps or Vortex agents. Abigail was relieved, but if there wasn't another way out, then they were doomed.

Riley touched Abigail's arm. "There's an inscription there. Can you read what it says?"

"It's hard to see," she said. "Can I use my flashlight?"

"It might not be safe," he said. "Maybe there are Vortex agents still in the tunnels behind us. Only use it as a last resort. Try to see if you can read it first."

She peered at the inscription and then said, "It's okay. I can read it. You know, maybe those Cretan architects did build this place after all. The inscription says, 'Beware the Minotaur'."

"Wasn't he half man, half bull? He lived in caves in Crete."

"Not in caves," Abigail corrected him. "In a labyrinth. If I were to guess, I'd say the inscription means we're about to enter a labyrinth."

"That doesn't sound good."

"No, it doesn't," Abigail agreed with a shudder.

"We could easily get lost. In the legend, Ariadne gave her lover, Theseus, a ball of twine so he wouldn't get lost in the labyrinth, but we don't have a ball of twine."

"So the reference isn't a clue?"

Abigail was confused. "What do you mean?"

"The Minotaur isn't a reference to something else, like to a passage in an ancient work that gives us a further clue?"

Abigail rubbed her forehead hard. "I doubt it. And if that's the case, then it's of absolutely no help, as I can't remember any ancient writings on the Minotaur. Except Plutarch," she added darkly.

Riley stepped closer. "Plutarch?"

"A biographer and historian who lived around the time the Book of Revelation was written. You won't like what he said about the Minotaur's labyrinth."

"Try me."

Abigail sighed and quoted,

> *"After wandering in the labyrinth,*
> *they could find no possible*
> *way out, so they ended their*
> *lives there in misery."*

"You're right," Riley said. "I don't like it. Look, we'll have to take things as they come. Let's go inside."

Abigail was reluctant to go into the tunnel, but Plutarch's words urged her forward. If they couldn't find an exit this way, then they would be trapped in there forever.

They were only fifty or steps into the tunnel when the tunnel branched into two. Each tunnel entrance had an inscription over it. "This inscription is from the first century," Abigail said. "Someone much later than Croesus found this temple. Maybe it was Bulut's ancestors."

"You can date it by looking at it?" Riley said.

"It's chapters and verses from the *Book of Revelation*," Abigail told him. "The *Book of Revelation* from the Bible was written around 96 AD, seven hundred years after Croesus."

"So it seems to me we're presented with a choice. One tunnel is booby-trapped and the other one isn't."

Abigail clutched her stomach in fear. "Or maybe they're both booby-trapped."

"Okay. So it seems the inscriptions were written at the end of the first century A.D. or later. Clearly, the treasure hasn't been stolen, so I'd hazard a guess that the tunnels were built by someone protecting the treasure and leaving instructions as to the safe way out."

"Maybe." Abigail's head was spinning. She wasn't sure that Riley was making any sense until the realization struck her. "Of course! Eymen's interest in the *Book of Revelation* and all the clues from the *Book of Revelation*! These inscriptions must have been left by Eymen Bulut's ancestors, the group protecting the copper scroll."

"Actually, I think you're right. What do the inscriptions say?"

"The inscription on the right says, 'Revelation Chapter 2 Verse 13', and the inscription on the left says, 'Revelation Chapter 2 Verse 14'."

"That's it?" Riley said, unable to keep the concern out of his voice. "We don't have a Bible on us. How do we know what the verses mean? I presume they offer clues as to what we'll meet inside the tunnels."

"I was raised Brethren," Abigail told him. "My parents were very strict and I had to memorize large portions of the Bible. I can't remember these verses word for word, but I am fairly sure that Verse 14 complains that some people follow the teaching of Balaam. That represents the tunnel on the right."

"And what about the tunnel on the left?" Riley asked her. "Verse 13?"

"That one says,

> *'I know where you dwell, where*
> *Satan's throne is. Yet you hold*
> *fast to my name, and you did*
> *not deny my faith.'"*

"Pergamon," Riley said without missing a beat.

"Yes, and that's written over the tunnel to the left."

"All right, so *Revelation* was speaking in a favorable manner about the people in verse 13, which is the tunnel on the left, and in an unfavorable manner about the people in verse 14, and that represents the tunnel on the right."

Abigail agreed, thinking it through as she spoke. "Yes. I think we're right about the clues. We have a choice of two tunnels, so we are making an educated guess that one is booby-trapped and the other one isn't. Verse 13 speaks about people favorably, whereas the other verse doesn't. On those grounds, I think we should take the tunnel on the left."

"We will still proceed carefully, just in case," Riley said.

Abigail was about to agree when the bright white light of a chem light burst behind them. Riley acted quickly, pulling Abigail into the darkness of the tunnel.

Abigail's heart was in her mouth. She knew they had no choice but to edge forward quickly without knowing what could be in front of them.

Just ahead of them, the tunnel took a right-angled turn to the left. Riley rounded the turn and then pulled Abigail around after him, holding her close to him.

They were so close she could feel his heart beating and his breath in her hair. She was trembling and he tightened his arms around her.

The man following her must be the man Riley had knocked unconscious, the man who had fallen next to her. Or maybe it was another man entirely. For all she knew, it was a whole army of men.

Over the sound of her beating heart, she could hear boots crunching. It did sound like only one man. Maybe if he took this tunnel, Riley would have the element of surprise. She jumped as a chem light flew into the tunnel, illuminating everything.

Abigail couldn't hear the man enter and she wondered if he had walked into the other tunnel.

All of a sudden, a scream rent the air.

"He's taken the other tunnel," Riley whispered in her ear. "Stay here. I'll be right back."

Abigail didn't want Riley to let her go. She felt safe in his arms despite being in such a predicament.

He detached from her and moved silently away. It was only after he had gone that Abigail wished she had told him to be careful in the tunnel.

Presently, he returned. "I didn't venture far inside the tunnel, but there was no sign of him."

"I'm glad you didn't go in," Abigail said. "There might have been a floor trap onto spikes or something."

"At least you know you chose the right tunnel," Riley said brightly.

Abigail forced a smile. "Let's hope both tunnels are not booby-trapped. I don't think they are, though," she added.

Riley tapped her elbow and urged her forward. "I think it's safe to use our flashlights, if not chem lights, at this point."

They crept along the tunnel shining their

flashlights over the rocks and the rubble on the ground.

Abigail was terrified that boiling oil would suddenly pour on their heads, even though she knew it wasn't a logical fear. She realized most fears weren't logical, but the notion afforded her no comfort.

For a few steps, Abigail thought they were climbing, and hoped they would come out onto the surface any minute. She was dismayed when their tunnel ended and their flashlights shone over the entrance to another two tunnels. Each had a verse from Revelation over it.

"The inscription over the tunnel on the left says 'Revelation Chapter 2 Verse 17' and over the tunnel on the right it says, 'Revelation Chapter 2 Verse 16'."

"What do they mean?" Riley said.

Abigail's mouth ran dry. "Um, I don't know," she stammered. "My mind has gone blank."

"That's understandable under the circumstances," Riley said. "Don't worry, it will come back to you. This is all a terrible shock."

Abigail nodded. She ran through the seven churches of Revelation in her mind. First the church of Ephesus, then Smyrna. Finally, she said aloud, "I've got it! Verse 16 is about the church of Pergamon. It says,

> 'So repent. If you do not, I will
> come to you soon and war
> against them with the sword
> of my mouth.'"

"So that's the tunnel to avoid," Riley said. "The tunnel to the right again. I assume Verse 17 is favorable?"

Abigail nodded and quoted the verse.

> "To the one who conquers I will
> give some of the hidden
> manna, and a white stone,
> with a new name written on
> the stone that nobody knows
> except the one who receives it."

"I don't pretend to understand that," Riley admitted, "except for the fact that it definitely seems favorable."

Abigail let out a long sigh of relief. "Thank goodness I remembered the verse. Yes, it looks like we go into the left tunnel again."

They stepped into the left tunnel, shining their flashlights over the tunnel walls and the ground. Immediately, something whizzed over Abigail's head.

"Bats again!" Riley said. "Are you all right?"

"Yes, fine." Abigail fervently wished for a breath of fresh air. "The bats smell pungent, and the tunnel air is no better."

"Bats are great news, though," Riley said. "Bats live at the entrance to caves. This surely means we're close to the exit."

The thought that she might be getting out of that place soon filled her with renewed hope. Maybe she would survive this after all. If only the tunnels remained wide enough for her to stand upright.

As they progressed further along the tunnel, there was an increasing amount of rubble on the ground. Abigail didn't know whether it was the result of earthquakes or simply the ravages of time. Riley helped her over the worst of the rubble. She went carefully, not wanting to twist an ankle.

"We're going up, although slowly," Riley said.

That's what Abigail had hoped. "Do you have any idea how far it would be to the surface?"

"Not a clue, but the bats give me hope."

"I hope there are no more tunnel choices," Abigail said, just as they rounded the corner and were met with two more tunnel entrances. She groaned aloud.

The inscription over the tunnel to the left said, 'Revelation 2:19' and the inscription over the tunnel to the left said, 'Revelation 2:20.'

Abigail rubbed her brow furiously. "Verse 20 is about Jezebel, I'm certain of it, but I can't quite remember what Verse 19 says."

Riley hurried to reassure her. "That's okay. We know the left tunnel is the tunnel we shouldn't go in, so this time we take the tunnel to the right."

"I'd better make sure," Abigail said. She shut her eyes tightly and then said. "Oh yes, I remember now. Verse 19 states,

> *'I know your actions, your love,*
> *faith, service, and patient*
> *endurance, and that your latter*
> *actions are better than your*
> *former actions.'"*

"Definitely favorable! The tunnel to the right it is."

Once more, they proceeded carefully along the

tunnel. Abigail hoped they wouldn't come across any more tunnels. She was also afraid the tunnels would circle and take them back to the Temple of Artemis. Still, no Vortex agents had appeared behind them, not since the man who had gone into the wrong tunnel.

As they continued, to Abigail's dismay, the tunnel became a little smaller, forcing Riley to stoop although Abigail could still stand upright.

"I can see light at the end of the tunnel," Riley said with a laugh.

"Are you sure?"

Abigail's eyes took a moment to adjust and then she said, "Yes, it does look a bit lighter there."

"Turn off your flashlight."

Abigail did as he said, and to her delight, he was right. There was a faint glow ahead. Abigail was so relieved, she was afraid she would burst into tears.

Her relief vanished in an instant when they moved toward the light and found themselves in a round pit. It had been made by human hands; Abigail estimated many centuries earlier.

A narrow hole was above their heads through which Abigail could see a narrow strip of blue sky.

Riley touched the walls. "It's like some kind of a well."

Abigail was aghast. "We'll never be able to climb up these walls!"

"We won't need to," Riley said. "There's a rope."

Abigail hadn't noticed the rope due to the vegetation and tree roots growing in the cracks between the stones.

Riley turned over the end of the rope in his hands. It was awfully thick.

Abigail looked at it askance. "I wonder how old it is. It doesn't look too good."

Riley pulled hard on it a couple times. "It looks secure enough," he said. "You go up first, and I'll catch you if you fall. Do you think you can make it?"

"I'm sure I can," Abigail said. They were deadly booby-traps and just as deadly Vortex agents behind her. Ahead was the surface. Abigail was going to make it up that rope one way or another. She only hoped the rope had been put there sometime after the first century B.C.

Abigail had thought it wasn't too far to the surface, but climbing up the rope, it felt ten times longer than she had estimated. Dirt and debris fell on her as she climbed. Her hands and shoulders ached and her legs felt like jelly. Finally, she managed to pull herself through the narrow opening at the top. There was a small tree nearby, the one, no doubt, whose roots were protruding through the pit walls. She grabbed it and hauled herself over to it, and then lay on her stomach, panting.

The bright sunlight forced Abigail to blink rapidly several times in succession. She gulped the fresh air. Abigail never wanted to see the inside of a cave again as long as she lived.

She looked around. It looked like any other bright sunny day on a pleasant Lydian hillside.

"Appearances can be deceptive," Abigail muttered to herself. She called down to Riley, "It looks perfectly safe. You can come up."

It was an anxious wait for Abigail. What if the rope wouldn't hold Riley's weight? At least she knew where he was and could fetch a rope from somewhere, but what if Vortex agents beat her to him?

To her relief, Riley climbed the rope quickly. He then pulled the rope from the pit. "That will stop anyone else coming up," he said with satisfaction. He looked around. "I wonder where the car is in relation to our present location?"

"The car? Wouldn't Vortex have slashed the tires or something like that?"

Riley shook his head. "No, because they'd leave it for Thatcher."

Abigail tapped herself on the side of the head. "Of course!"

"We will have to go carefully. There could be more Vortex agents about," Riley said, looking at his watch.

It took Abigail a moment or two to realize his watch was also a compass.

Abigail followed Riley to the top of a sheer rock face. She wished she could feel relieved, but wasn't going to allow herself the feeling until she was safely in a hotel room, or maybe even back home. All her life she had wanted adventure, but now was thinking that maybe adventure was overrated.

Riley pointed to the dirt road just below them. Abigail couldn't see the car from her position, but she had a good idea where it was. Now, if only she could manage to avoid being shot.

They turned around.

Abigail gasped at the sight before her. It couldn't be true!

SARDIS: ANCIENT SITE

A MAN WAS STANDING THERE, SILHOUETTED BY the brilliant white glare of the sun.

As Abigail's eyes adjusted, she saw the man was Berat. He was holding a gun.

Riley pushed Abigail behind him.

"Isn't this a stroke of luck!" Berat said. "Imagine finding you two here. Where are your two friends?"

Riley held up both hands, palms outward. "They're both dead. Look, we're on the same side here. There are agents from the covert organization

I told you about in the Temple to Artemis right now. They followed us inside. My agency is trying to cover up the existence of the treasure."

Berat uttered a harsh laugh. "Do I look like I was born yesterday? I'm not stupid. Your government wants to get their hands on the treasure."

Riley hurried to assure him otherwise. "I work for an international organization that wants to stop valuable relics falling into the wrong hands."

Abigail peeked out from behind Riley. Berat looked hesitant. Did he possibly believe them?

Berat gestured into the pit. "Is there anyone alive down there?"

"Not close to the pit as far as I know," Riley told him, "but I can't be sure. We were attacked."

Berat dropped something into the pit. He waved the gun and gestured that they move to a position behind some rocks. Abigail took that as a good sign —Berat hadn't shot them yet.

The ground shook. Abigail staggered and Riley put out his hand to steady her.

"The pit has caved in now. Nobody will ever find that entrance." Berat raised his gun.

"You're not a bad man," Riley said. "You don't want to shoot innocent people. Our mission was to hide the treasure and now it's hidden. We're on the same side."

Berat appeared to be thinking it over. After what seemed to Abigail to be an age, he said, "That might be true, but I can't take any chances."

"At least let the woman go," Riley said. "She's an academic. She most certainly doesn't want anyone finding the treasure. Check our pockets; you can see we haven't taken any of the gold."

As he spoke, Abigail saw a figure creeping up behind Berat. It was Ellis.

She did her best not to gasp and stare at him. She tried to focus on Berat while watching Ellis out of her peripheral vision.

Was Ellis working for Vortex? She didn't think so. Thatcher had been, and he told them he had done away with Ellis. She supposed she would find out soon enough.

It was over in a flash. Ellis jumped on top of Berat. The gun went off, causing little bits of stone from a nearby rock face to shatter over Abigail's face. She put her hands over her eyes. When she took her hands away, Ellis had disarmed Berat and was standing over him holding Berat's gun.

"Ellis!" Riley exclaimed. "We thought you were dead."

Ellis put his hand behind his head and pulled it away, holding it out for Abigail and Riley to see. It was covered with blood. "Thatcher hit me hard over the back of the head. I've probably got a concussion. I must've been out cold for a while." He hesitated before adding, "At least I think it was Thatcher. I was with him when I was hit from behind."

Riley gave him a nod of affirmation. "Yes, it was Thatcher. He was working for Vortex."

Ellis shook his head and then clutched it with both hands. "Ouch! I had no idea. I should have seen it coming."

"We *both* should have seen it coming," Riley said. "How did you find us?"

"When I came to, I heard an explosion, and I saw this man heading up the hills. I figured he was responsible for the explosion, so I thought I should follow him."

"Just as well you did!" Abigail said.

Ellis afforded her a thin smile. He pulled Berat to his feet. "What are we going to do with him? I take it he's not working for Vortex?"

"No, but Thatcher had called other agents. There were Vortex agents in there," Riley said.

"You can let me go," Berat said. "I only want to protect the treasure and I've already done that."

"There was no treasure in there," Riley said.

Abigail did her best not to look shocked at his statement.

"It was obviously looted centuries ago," Riley continued.

Berat gasped. "What? No treasure? But you said…"

"Not so much as a small gold brooch," Abigail said, catching onto Riley's intent to keep Ellis out of the loop. "Looters had obviously removed it all at some point over the centuries."

"But how?" Berat said. "It was booby-trapped."

"We got out of there, didn't we?" Riley said. "Obviously, the booby-traps were removed by the looters."

Abigail studied Berat's face to see if he would believe them.

Riley pushed on. "Still, it *is* a significant archeological find. We need to keep it safe. It would be terrible if the Temple of Artemis was removed and placed in a museum."

"Yes, it's a perfectly intact piece of architecture," Abigail said. "It's magnificent. If any archeological team found it, they could damage it in the excavation. Don't forget, the Altar of Zeus at Pergamon is now in a museum in Berlin. Only the podium remains at Pergamum. I'd hate that happen to the Temple of Artemis."

Berat appeared to be digesting their words. "Maybe the treasure your ancestors wanted you to guard was the ancient architecture itself," Abigail added.

Berat shook his head vigorously. "No, it was the Croesus treasure. I'm certain of that."

Abigail waved one hand at him in dismissal. "The treasure is long gone. Only the temple remains."

"Look, you have a choice," Riley told him. "Either we take you and throw you in prison where you will never see the light of day or…"

Berat interrupted him. "You can't. What would you arrest me for? Illegally discharging explosives? I'd be out of prison in no time."

Riley shook his head. "You won't have a trial. You will be in a *special* prison, one provided by my government."

"What my associate is trying to say but is putting in a nice way," Ellis told him, "is either we shoot you now and leave you here for the vultures, or we imprison you for years, or you can go back to your home and continue to guard the whereabouts of the location."

"What's there to guard?" Berat spat.

Riley stepped forward. "If you feel that way, you can choose one of the first two options."

Ellis held the gun against Berat's head. "Why even give him options? He might talk. We don't need him alive."

"Yes, we do," Riley countered. "If he goes missing, Vortex might make the connection between him and Eymen. They're already aware of Murat's connection. Obviously, his organization goes deeper than what he's told us. It's in our interests to protect them, as they will protect this site."

"Who cares about the site?" Ellis said. "There's no treasure."

Abigail stepped forward. "*I* care about the site. It has massive archeological significance. It must be protected."

A look of realization passed over Berat's face. Abigail figured it finally occurred to him that Riley did not want Ellis to know about the treasure. In that instant, Abigail could see Berat now trusted Riley.

Berat nodded to Riley and winked at Abigail. "We have an understanding. Murat and our associates and I will continue to prevent anyone from finding the location. Do we need to hide from those agents?"

Riley shook his head. "I doubt it. I think they're all in there." He pointed to the ground.

Ellis pursed his lips. "You're going to let him go?"

Riley shot him a quelling look. Ellis looked away, but not before he said, "Go on, Berat. Keep in front of me at all times. I'll give your gun back to you when we reach your car."

Riley helped Abigail over the rough going down the hill. She probably didn't need his help, but she was grateful for it, nonetheless. They kept to the dubious cover of the sparse trees dotting the hillside, and kept a careful eye out for Vortex agents, despite the fact Riley doubted there were any survivors.

Abigail touched Riley's arm and brought him to a standstill. "I don't see any vehicles," she said. She looked out over the plains where once, thousands of years ago, the lower city of Sardis had stood, housing the reed huts of the poor people who were living close to the rich gold deposits of the river. It was ironic, she thought.

He looked surprised. "What do you mean?"

"The Vortex agents. How they many of them were there? There must have been at least one car."

Riley pointed down by the banks of the Pactolus River.

It took Abigail a while to see it. The SUV was well camouflaged against the rocks. "I hope there's no one in it," she said.

"They were all inside the mountain when I blew up the entrance," Berat told them in a matter-of-fact voice. "I watched you arrive, and saw them too. I was posing as a tourist with a telephoto lens on my camera. I knew you would turn up at Sardis sooner or later."

There was merely a short rocky scramble and then they were down the hill. Riley lowered himself over the ledge and then signaled for Abigail to jump.

She did so, and landed hard in Riley's arms. He kept his arms around her for longer than he should have, judging by Ellis's dour expression.

"What now?" Abigail asked Riley when he finally released her.

"We go home."

PENNSYLVANIA

ABIGAIL WALKED BACK TO HER OFFICE. HER PAPER had been well received. Even the question time had gone well. Her part in the conference was over; now she could relax.

She unlocked her door, entered her office, and took off her shoes. She walked over to her desk, spun her chair so it swiveled a few times, and then put her feet up on the desk and wiggled her toes.

Abigail had loved being an academic, but now she'd had more than a little taste of excitement and adventure. And as terrified as she had been at the time, she already missed it.

And where was Riley? He had been conspicuous by his absence. Was she only going to see him on missions? The thought saddened her.

There was a knock on the door and Abigail at once took her feet off the desk. "Come in," she called out.

To her dismay, in stepped Professor Harvey Hamilton, his face flushed. "Your paper went well." He said it almost as an accusation.

Abigail shot him a bright smile. "Thank you."

"I thought I would offer you my congratulations before I give my paper tonight."

"I hope it goes well. Best of luck."

He narrowed his eyes. "Thank you. So, after the conference is over tomorrow, all the faculty members are having dinner with the visiting academics."

Abigail nodded. "That's right. I haven't forgotten."

Hamilton gave a small nod and made to walk out, his hand resting on the door. "So you're not going to dispute being part-time?"

"Dispute?" Abigail repeated.

He shot her an irritated look. "You're not going

to take it higher than the Dean?"

Abigail laughed. "No. I'm happy with part-time. It gives me time for my other interests." *Like relic hunting in exotic locations*, she silently added.

"Oh yes. Baking and quilting with your Amish friends."

"Something like that."

Professor Hamilton nodded once more and shut the door.

Abigail put her feet back on the desk and laced her fingers behind her head. So that's why Hamilton had come. It was out of character for him to congratulate her on her paper. Clearly, his purpose in coming was to ascertain whether she was going to contest the Dean's decision. And why did he ask about tomorrow night's dinner? Upon reflection, Abigail figured it was because he wanted to make sure she wasn't having dinner with any of the visiting academics in person. Hamilton was quite competitive academically.

Abigail smiled to herself. He could ingratiate himself to as many visiting academics as he liked. She didn't care about such things.

There was another knock on the door. Abigail wondered what Hamilton had forgotten. Once more, she removed her feet from her desk. "Come in," she called again, steeling herself for another encounter.

To her shock, Riley was in the doorway. "Riley!" she exclaimed, standing up. "I didn't expect to see you." She tried not to look too pleased.

He walked inside and shut the door.

"Do we have another mission?"

Riley looked somewhat taken aback. "No. I came to ask you a question."

Abigail's spirits fell. He had come simply to ask her a question? It must be important. And for a moment she had thought he was there to see her. "What is it?

"After all your experiences in Turkey, do you still like Turkish delight?"

Abigail frowned hard. What sort of question was that? "Yes, I do," she said hesitantly.

"And do you have any plans for tonight?"

She smiled at him. "That's two questions."

"I know a little Turkish restaurant not far from here," Riley said, offering her his arm. "Would you care to have dinner with me?"

"That's three questions," Abigail said as she took Riley's arm and accompanied him out the door.

NEXT BOOK IN THIS SERIES

Goliath's spear has allegedly come to light, and Abigail and Riley are sent to investigate. Before they arrive in Cairo, the spear goes missing.

Abigail and Riley must decipher the code in a three thousand year old Egyptian papyrus while avoiding ruthless agents who will stop at nothing to guard the secrets of the spear.

ABOUT RUTH HARTZLER

USA Today best-selling author Ruth Hartzler spends her days writing, walking her dog, and thinking of ways to murder somebody. That's because Ruth writes mysteries and thrillers.

She is best known for her archeological thrillers, for which she relies upon her former career as a college professor of ancient languages and Biblical history.

Made in the
USA
Monee, IL